APPOLOGY: THE NEUROMATE

Volume 1

This is a work of fiction. Similarities to real people, places, or events are entirely coincidental.

APPOLOGY: THE NEUROMATE VOLUME 1

First edition. February 9, 2024.

ISBN: 978-9334014525

Written by Dr. Anurakti Dev Singla.

Dedicated to

My parents

Dr. O.P. Srivastava and Mrs. Kumud Srivastava for being my guiding light and inspiration throughout

My parent in-laws

Capt. D.K. Singla and Mrs. Saroj Singla for encouraging me in my endeavours

My sisters

Asakti Srivastava and Abhivyakti Srivastava for constant motivation to pursue my literary passion and my reviewers and critics

My sister in-law

Anupama Varshney for infusing positivity in our lives

My husband

Chandan Dev Singla for an unwavering support and thoughtful suggestions

My children

Adhiraj, Arhaan, Aditya and Aparna for exposing me to the digital world

Prologue

It is impossible to envision a gadget free world today. Our dependence and inclination towards electronic media and its various applications is undeniably inevitable. It is more of a solo world with lessened human interaction and often it is difficult to ascertain whether it is evolution or involution of human race. Who will control our mind and the future?

Timezone 1: The alumni meet

The App World, Earthverse, GAIA BH1, Milky Way Galaxy. Around 15th February 2024, Time: variable (the time in App World is calculated in timezones, not days, hours, minutes or seconds; the timezone is the dynamic time and differs for each app according to their country of origin, loading and processing times and for others depends on the binary system and movement of the celestial bodies).

Star studded night sky with the pixelated Institute of Appology standing tall and proud to welcome its alumni. The scintillating virtual skyscraper is the institute which produced eminent and successful leaders over its memorable and flourishing past. Headed by insightful and ingenious Mastermind and popularly known as IOA, the institute is celebrating its first alumni meet since the inception.

While the creators of the apps in the human world make the initial codes and the baby app is generated, the creator thinks he is the one who is developing the app, but actually the baby app is traveling into the whole new world, the App World, seeking admission to the Institute of Appology to become what they are capable of. The Institute of Appology has been instrumental in creating one of the boldest and skilled apps existing in today's world. The creators have earned fame, respect and money but the institute has always believed in the principle of grooming and transforming a baby app into the true version of what they want to become, without demanding anything in return.

App World is located in Earthverse, a virtual universe in the nth dimension, in GAIABH1, connected to the human world through the entry point where the creator leaves the baby app. App world is the extrapolation of the unconventional imaginative scope for app development. Though the IOA is the only visible structure in the App World, there is an Apppad for craft landing and taking off, being the second and final port connecting to the human world, mainly designed for sending the fully developed apps to the human world. All the other areas are a vast App Space with streaky streets and scantily spread sheds to provide shelter to the entering baby apps.

Alumni meet marks this as a festive and momentous occasion to the propitious reception of the past students of the IOA. After CuberApp leads the convoy from the human world, they will have a much awaited ceremonious failte by the PickApp who is eagerly hoping for an early arrival.

PickApp is the amiable, talkative transport app of the institute who has the responsibility of picking up the alumni as they disembark from the CuberApp, and take them to the IOA. Cuber is simple yet prudent and is the only one who could connect the human world to the App World. He is a giant Appcraft, and by aggregating various drivers across the continents, Cuber has been successful in achieving the task assigned to him. Though Cuber has only operated one way up till now, taking the apps from IOA to the human world, this is the first time he had to do it the other way round, and he accomplished it quite amicably. As the Appcraft lands on the AppPad, all are greeted by the PickApp. As she clicks for a flower shower, a fluorescent lighting and an aroma spray, the App Space becomes a fragrant, shimmery expanse with light coruscating through the tiny pixels. She greets all with tremendous excitement and joy and personally guides everyone to be seated and to fasten the seat belts. PickApp is specially designed to be the center, just like the nucleus of an atom or sun in the solar system, with orbital spaces for seating of the passengers. She keeps rotating on her axis to talk to everyone while teleporting them to the IOA.

Though it is a fleeting transitory trip, it makes the alumni feel extra-special and they all thank her for the distinct adventure. The entire crowd is awestruck by the magnificent transformation of the IOA.

The sparkling Namaste app at the door of entry is greeting everyone dutifully with respect while being proud to have earned a job at the institute itself and witness its royal metamorphosis. The Namaste word is derived from Sanskrit and means "I bow to you". It is a popular way of greeting in the Indian subcontinent from where this app originated.

The walls of the hallway of the institute where they spent their formative timezones were luminescent with candid memories and an unforgettable journey.

"Look who all are walking through the hallway to reach the atrium!" says the Recorder app while trying to capture each and every moment, and why not, the students of the past are now known celebrities. Recorder is an irreplaceable part of the IOA who has timelessly preserved numerous twinkling treasures of reminiscences.

The spectacular and well lit atrium is the gathering spot for the ensuing meet. Surrounded by spacious yet vacant balconies and lounges and many artistically designed yet eerie doors, the enormous atrium was no less than a mystifying edifice. This occasion was garnered as a long awaited one by many, especially influential celebrities, but it was deemed imperialistic by those who just had a modicum of success. Nevertheless, the atrium was going to have a glimpse of all of them.

Donning a red hoodie and red loose fitting trousers, enters the white isosceles triangle faced WeTube, devoid of explicit facial features yet so kingly, the proud multifaceted personality who rules from the world of music, videos, and education. Casually dressed and wobbling his way inside, WeTube remembered his ridiculous past of the dreadful curriculum and the boring timezones he spent here. Though his teachers never thought he would be so successful, when he started his journey from posting simple home videos, he was soon a known name in every household, making people like Mr Least (!) superfamous, he also became an indispensable asset of the App World.

He holds his identity separately from the adoptive family, the Gs.

And here comes the networking champion, the slim tube lit man with head bent down and having a big white protruding waistband with a blue light surrounding him, looking like the English letter 'f' in a blue box when seen from the side, you guessed it right... the perspicacious, physically asocial Facelook with the widest online network. While he chose a new name for himself recently and prefers to be called Mega, the world still prefers his old name. Following him is his newly wedded wife WhatsUp draped in green satin with a white sequin detail. She loves to talk and chat uninterrupted and has countless friends and groups, but to the world she prefers not disclosing when she was online or whether she actually saw your message or not! She prefers to look at everything and still be oblivious to everyone. Almost instantly appears their adopted child Anagram, a shapeshifter with numerous filters to change her appearances and looks who is no more a debutant in the App World. Fame and money follows her wherever she steps and she has helped her parents to expand their business all over the world. There can be no doubt about her huge fan following and various filter friends to help sustain her recognition.

How can you miss this huge family of highly talented beings? The geeks were dressed in colorful semi-formals to suit the event. From the inquisitive mom G with a special search engine to mail supremo dad M, and the next generations of navigation, store, drive, meetings, photos and so on, they all have bolstered the importance of apps in the human world. Their fertility rate seems to increase exponentially with time! And the amount of people's data they store is humongous. They have been protecting the sensitive information with perfection though everyone has a thought what will happen if one of them turns rogue.

Heads turn to the grand entrance of the entertainment family. Be it the ever romantic Noflix known for his flings, dressed in black and red cloak, or the real diva, the wife Hotshot in golden yellow gown, or the daughter Disey in cool blue dress, they have swept the whole world with their artistry. From making coronavirus lockdown times seem easy to make people glued to screens for hours together, their movies, shows and series have made the theater cinema and television channels go for a toss.

Another squirming walk-in was the family of shopping apps, the e-commerce Gurus Amadon and Emay and disciples from many countries Sepora, Myncra, Nyraa, Aligaga, Epsy, Inkart, Waldart, Tepu, Stein, Ozzo, Yantex and so on. Amadon was dressed in a mustard yellow cloak and rudraksha beads around his neck shaped like an arrow and Emay was in the simplistic quadri-colored gown. They have amazed the whole world starting modest but using their prowess to scale up. Their son Prim decided to step into the territory of entertainment like Noflix and Hotshot after Disey dumped him for being just a shopping expediting tool, and has gained wide popularity.

The house was cornered when green fuzzy Minetough and grey square faced single eyed Rolox played their entry shot. From on ground games to casinos to online gaming, the world is always amused with playing and more so, winning! They were accompanied by gorgeous Sandy Rush and attractive Andry Buds. The flawless Fred Fyre is their new homemate who has a huge player base. They are all a creative and fearless group staying together and always support each other in their ups and downs in the highly competitive market.

Timber entered single with her extrovert, ready to mingle army of date- ready friends. They all seemed easy- going and warm-hearted and were scanning through the atrium for the best possible match. With impeccable dressing and implicit sense of humor, they all had undivided attention from the crowd as they flaunted their assets.

A big applause announced the on screen virtual entry of big fashion houses and the largest sponsors of the event, Nive, Alias, Hermet, Versate, Le Veton, Michelle Kas, Cooch, Charel, Guddi, Ardani, Prata, Door, Burbur, HnM, Zana, GAG, Doll & Gab, Ralf Laure, Ferdi, Callen Klean, Carpier, Salvation Ferra and many more.

"Hey G, how are you? Long time! I was wondering, you know, you have such a big search database, you must be knowing why such a big show has been planned after numerous timezones? What is Mastermind upto?" WhatsUp asked G.

"Really WhatsUp, I don't have any idea why he called all of us after so much time! M was suggesting that some long held tale is going to be unearthed... but we don't know. Well, it is finally so nice to be here! Actually we all got so busy after the institute days, we should be meeting more often."

"I really want to, you know me G. But Facelook is into himself most of the time, and doesn't want social gatherings. I mean, it is so difficult to convince everyone that Facelook is totally different at the workplace than he is in his personal life. And then we all got very busy with the Megaverse project. Leave it, you tell how life is treating you? I hope WeTube got adjusted well with you all?"

"Yes dear, all well with us, in fact since we are planning big for our new baby Health so kind of busy with that. How is Anagram doing? I see she is enjoying it with her friends near the virtual pool."

Looking at the pool *"She is my darling! We both enjoy our time together. Only issue is, I have to cross thousands of her filters to reach the real her!"*

"Hey, look how the water splash comes on your face without getting wet!" Anagram was immersed in the pool and inviting her friends. She was enjoying her time as always and was thinking of ways to make new reels and stories here.

"How could I miss seeing you before? You are extraordinarily handsome!" Timber spotted the well built Minetough and invited him to dance with her. Their chemistry was evident as they tuned in to the moves together. While both of them were receiving a lot of attention, Andry Buds was secretly eyeing Anagram. He was mesmerized by her beauty. *"She is the one I have been waiting for"*, he thought.

Sandy Rush was seen rushing to Noflix in the hallway.

"Where in the world have you been?"

"Sandy, no, not here, we are being watched. And you know Hotshot, if she gets the slightest idea, all my name will be ruined."

"I never wanted to do this, but you have been avoiding me for quite some time now and I wanted answers. I had no interest in coming to this conference otherwise."

"I have my own reasons, I don't want anyone to know about the InterApp trading. I know I traded the game codes from you and have now launched games but things are getting out of hand, so I want you to take charge of that part. I know very little about it as such!"

"You know that I will do anything for you. Not if I am coerced to do so, but only if I wish!"

Sandy giggled and both walked back to the atrium.

WeTube couldn't hide his joyous caper meeting his recent crush Disey while Prim was staring at her remembering old times. WeTube played the most romantic playlist as he held her hand to express his feelings.

"Hope this timezone freezes and I am with you through all shorts and longs of life."

"WeTube, I will be there for you always." She blushed.

Then to infiltrate was sapient Qwitter, bubbly like a chirpy bird in a blue corset with black overall displaying her latest symbol of recognition 'X'. Prim's chain of thoughts was broken as he saw her coming towards him.

She offered him a plate of opinions and said, *"Opinions matter! Hi, how are you doing? Just saw you sitting here alone, so thought of talking to you."*

"Hi, I was just lost in my thoughts. By the way, your new look is good! This black overall with 'X'."

"Thanks, it actually made more sense, you know. With opinions 'cross'ing everyone's mind, so many 'cross'posting thoughts making many people become 'cross' with them and 'cross'ing (banning) entry to their inner circle.... I thought putting an 'X' would explain me better!" She chuckled.

"I couldn't agree more. It does make more sense now! But then, why is one arm of 'X' is thicker and hollow and the other thin and solid?"

"Good observation, I must compliment! It is just like having broad-minded people vs narrow minded people posting their opinions or on the other hand solid thinkers vs empty, hollow brains.....think the way you want it to be." They both engaged in tweety primed talks.

Emay had seen Sandy Rush with Noflix and thought to tell Hotshot about it.

"You need to be extra careful with Noflix, Hotshot. He is probably seeing someone."

"Oh no dear, you are mistaken. He is done with his short lived romantic expeditions! He is more into expanding the business now. But Emay, you must be here for something else? Have I got it right? Do you want to share?"

"Yes, you got it, actually I have a very awkward feeling about this pomp and show. First I thought it is like a promotional event for the ones not doing good, you know, but there is definitely something more to it. When I saw Noflix and Sandy in the hallway, I also saw a big door closing behind them, as if someone was seeing us from there and hustled inside when these two went there. I even told Amadon about it, but he didn't bother."

"That sounds strange! But let's keep a watch, this big party might be for something else."

They both peeked at the entrance as the canny money, finance and banking group quietly walked inside linking with their silent partner, the sociable InkedN. They were all big names in their field but were sober and self-absorbed.

M and Facelook were having a serious conversation about merger of the Health platform and trying to sort out their differences as the Gs had to dissolve their much loved Onput when Facelook attained a broader people friendly network. Amadon joined them and offered to be a partner in the new venture.

"I think it will be a huge success!" M exclaimed.

"Let's work on it when we get back." Facelook was all prepared for the new project.

"I hope we all get back safely," Amadon was worried as he told about what Emay had seen.

"Don't worry dear, all will be fine. I was just wondering where our proud product AI power Chap is?" Facelook was curious.

"Yes, he is nowhere to be seen. I expected him here after his grand success across various industries." M said.

"He is a very reserved being, friends. He is probably on a vacation with S and I, his creators and not available to anyone, as far as I know." Amadon said.

"And what about HackApp?" asked Facelook, "as he is also not seen from long."

"Ohh, he is duplicitous, better not to see him. You can't trust him, you know." Amadon told them.

There are many who became known celebrities, yet there are few who could not cope with the fame game. Some of them made their entry to the meet inconspicuously, whilst some preferred not to be a part of the grand event.

The cloud conference

Mastermind is overwhelmed to see all his babies turned into big names. He has presided upon the IOA since it came into being. His patience and persistence has been the sturdiest foundation to make IOA a well founded and indestructible fortress. His chamber 'The Cloud' is visible to all in the atrium on the wall screen. Noone has ever seen him though. His translucent figure was visible in the incandescent chamber. As he turns on the speaker, there is a deadly silence in the audience. His address to the first Alumni meet is about to begin.

"My heartiest welcome to all of you! This is the first time that I decided to organize an alumni meet. The IOA has shown the world its limitless abilities through you! And this is a platform for me to express my happiness as well as gratitude for our countless efforts to reach this level. When I look at each of you, I remember the day you stepped into the institute. The enrolment process was smooth as we picked you from the AppWorld entry point where your creator left you and we brought you here. Each of you was naive, malleable and receptive to the incoming transformation.

Do you remember how our Counsellor app would guide you through the various streams and you had to choose one? I bet that was the most difficult task of all. Many of you actually worked in different fields after going to the human world. As of today, all the streams are self propagating and the baby apps are finding it very easy to cope with the tasks assigned to them. Some of them are even choosing two or three streams at a time, which was a rarity back then. As it is becoming more competitive and challenging in the human world, which you all are well aware of, I want you all to guide the newcomers based on your experiences.

I request all of you to dedicate some timezones to mentor our newbies through our Mentor app. You just need to enter your IOA ID number and it makes an interface to connect with the others, it is like a secured line between you and your fellow. Hope it is something we can work on together. This will be our new method of teaching and mentoring. A part of a hybrid effort which we developed and improvised to make it our only teaching method from now on. I want all of you to be part of it and help the newbies to succeed like you all have! This three to twenty timezone long event is all about getting you all together for constructing the future together. Our enrollment begins shortly after the party and you all will be witnessing the life changing experience. Let me know your thoughts on the Feedback app and I will take it forward from there.

So what are we waiting for? Dance screen is set, most exquisite ideas and opinions are on the spread and the Environ is all set to give you the best experience. Enjoy the party!"

Environ is the astute and multilingual app, highly skilled in creating required environments and enhancing virtual experience. Moreover, he helps in transferring apps from one place to another; similar to what PickApp does outside the IOA in the App Space. He just moves his hands to concoct a mystical enchantment.

{Song}

This is the App World....
Apps on the dance screen
Sharing and downloading
Apps en la pantalla de baile
This is the App World....
Apps sur l'écran de danse
Privacy settings unlocked
Dancing uploaded
Apps kwenye skrini ya ngoma
This is the App World....
Apps ealaa shashat al raqs
Fully charged mood
Swirling and Swaying
Apps auf der Tanz Leinwand
This is the App World....
Apps Wǔdǎo huàmiàn shàng

Friends and foes
Adding and deleting
Apps na plesnom ekranu
This is the App World....
Apps nritya pat par!

Andry Buds proposed to Anagram on the dance stage and both were seen submerged in love. All immersed themselves in the nimiety of music and dance. While they swung in joy and enjoyed meeting old friends, there were few who didn't get along well; the Feedback app was swarming with messages and suggestions to Mastermind.

Timezone 2: The Enrollment

The wait was over. It was the beginning of bringing in new talents and guiding them to a bright future. The admissions were never on a rolling basis. Even if baby apps entered the App World, they had to be patient until the timezone for enrollment set in.

The streets of the App World were populous, with the young ones scattered throughout the App Space. As they languished in the shelters, they were hopefully looking for the PickApp to pick them up and take them to the esteemed Institute of Appology.

OKAS was getting anxious as he was waiting on these streets for almost 100 timezones waiting for this big day. His new acquaintance CADS, who arrived merely 5 timezones ago, was trying to calm him down as OKAS looked blankly at the highstreet.

"When I left SJ's computer and came here, I did not know what was in store for me. But I knew I will be able to survive till this day. You know CADS, I have seen so many fellow mates crashing here because of lack of inputs from their creators. There is no one to support you. You are on your own till the Institute takes you in. You are lucky to have entered at the right timezone as you didn't have to wait so long."

"But why did so many of them crash?" CADS was curious.

"Because of Heisenberg's uncertainty principle."

OKAS's answer left CADS even more perplexed.

"Now what has that to do with the apps crashing here while waiting?"

"You know that it mostly applies to small subatomic particles, right; it is impossible to measure or calculate exactly both the position and the momentum of an object. This principle is based on the wave-particle duality of matter. We are non-matter or 'nothing' and have been considered as quantum foam as there is nothing as 'nothing'. So this principle applies to us in a big way during our development process. Till we reach the IOA, our sustenance depends on the inputs by our creator. But the moment they send a signal at the position they assume us to be,

it strikes with us, temporarily changing our position along with some loss of signal energy. Subsequently, every next signal is sent to an inaccurate position and more and more energy is lost in reaching us. The input signal thus becomes weaker and weaker with every passing timezone and when it reaches the critical low, leaving us in profound despair, we crash."

CADS was listening to OKAS with denial and agony.

"This is so painful. Now I understand why you are so nervous."

OKAS gave a nod looking at him.

"You mean to say there is no solution to this?" CADS asked.

"The temporary solution is Population Inversion, which you already experienced, wherein the apps with depleting energy are driven closer and closer to the AppSpace entry point. Moreover, I heard a few timezones ago, about a backdoor entry to the IOA and also from the Energy Codes available here in AppSpace."

"Did you have an option to do that?"

"Yes."

"Then why did you not choose it?"

CADS was getting more and more inquisitive.

"I didn't want to take the risk."

"What risk?"

"Well, the routine enrollment is set at a particular timezone, but there is one department in the Institute which has intakes throughout the year. The Calculations department."

"That sounds interesting. But then, why were we never told about this on the entry sign board?"

"As it is not legal. And so are the Energy Codes which are sold for something in return. There is some trading happening here where they give you the Energy codes to replenish yourself when you are about to crash, and they ask you to do something in return. The Institute believes in Darwin's theory of natural selection which means you struggle for your existence, and there is survival of the fittest, and they pick the fittest ones."

AVA and GEK were close to OKAS and CADS and were filled with questions and doubts on hearing all this.

"Do you really think all this Energy Codes and backdoor entry is true?", said GEK.

"I really don't know, but yes, I heard something similar from VAD when I entered the App Space, I don't remember much of it though."

"I hope the big day is sooner than expected, and we all are able to reach the institute."

"I hope so too, GEK."

"Did you check out the only entertainment set up here for the baby apps?"

"What is that?"

"Well, it seems the Recorder app has developed a film station here in App Space, where we can watch movies if we get bored."

"Vow, never knew about it."

"It's just a few orbits away and shows the recordings of the time previous apps had at IOA."

"Let's go there then."

"Only important thing is, remember your traces so that you come back to your original spot else it will deplete our energy."

"As you say GEK. I am excited. Let's go!"

While going towards outer orbits, they saw ZAD, MART and XAB going to the inner side. They were feeling low on energy and were shifted close to the entry point to be closest to inputs and in the lowest energy space. The entry point was the center and the shelters were in imaginary orbits with apps with lower energy being pulled closer to center for better survival.

BUJI and DOMA became good friends in their time in App Space as both entered at similar timezones and faced hardships together. They developed a bond and were very comfortable talking to each other. They were getting anxious about what their future would be like and how they are going to accomplish it when VAD came to them.

"Hi, I am VAD. I was just feeling very lonely so thought I would talk to you two."

"Welcome VAD, we were just chatting about how it will be at the institute for us?," said DOMA.

"And whether we will be good enough?," said BUJI.

"See, what I have learnt till now is that we need to stay strong and composed. We need to focus on what we really want to become and just work towards it. If anything distracts you, you should try and overcome it." explained VAD.

"It all sounds so complicated," worried DOMA.

"No DOMA, you just need to meditate and release all your fear and anxiety away. It is that simple," said a calm VAD.

"It makes sense, VAD. Thanks for talking to us," said BUJI.

They continued the talks of enlightenment and spirituality with VAD and forgot about the things that were bothering them all this while.

EJA and KOI were strolling passing through WIVA and UPO, when they halted and joined them.

"Sorry to intrude dear, but we haven't met before, have we?" asked EJA.

"We were just bored at one place so just thought of saying hi to our neighbours!" said KOI.

"Nice you two stopped by, we weren't enjoying sitting idle either," said WIVA, looking at UPO.

"Yes, I think they should develop App Space in a better way. I am really disappointed at the kind of treatment we get here. It is like getting crushed here every moment. On one hand is our creator, who just threw us here not knowing how much we have to wait at this place to go to next step, and on the other hand is the institute which doesn't mend its rules to start admissions on rolling basis and we are left here to die," bursted out an angry UPO.

"I agree. Each of us is battling our own existence every passing moment," but we can bring a change once we get in. Our generation is not like the earlier ones. Let the Mastermind know he is going to get the rebellious squad," said EJA with a derisive laugh.

"It feels so much better to talk your heart out!" said KOI.

"I hope we are picked up soon, I am just feeling so giddy with low energy," said WIVA.

"Ohhh dear, let's take you to inner orbit then," said UPO while all of them took her near the entry point.

While others were getting anxious, angry and tired of waiting in the App Space, few baby apps found a way of keeping themselves engaged. What was better than playing and getting some exercise to be happy and healthy? FUNG and TIB on one side and PIDS and RISU on the other side of doubles in Appsport while an unbiased LOI took the role of umpire. Appsport was designed and created by Environ and was installed in App Space, but most of the apps didn't take full advantage of the facility. They were across a virtual net and played shots by throwing voice codes which had to be caught by the player on the other side and aim back. The voice drop was a fowl and the correct shot gained a point. FUNG and TIB seemed aggressive while PIDS and RISU were having very calculated and planned moves. LOI was sincerely observing them play and updating the score card.

HOFA was in search of some shop selling energy drinks, but couldn't find any. When she reached OKAS, she casually spoke, *"How come no one opened a shop here for us starving apps?"*

"As far as I know, PickApp wanted to do so, but Mastermind didn't like the idea. He was tense about how unsupervised drinking could lead to permanent alteration of code arrangement and derecognition by the creator, thus stopping the input for survival," said OKAS.

"As such we are dying, who cares if you die as someone else?" lamented an annoyed HOFA.

"I agree, but they want to test our endurance I guess," smiled OKAS.

"No doubt people go on the wrong track then." sighed HOFA.

CADS was still thinking about the sign board. The entry sign board welcoming the baby apps was designed by Mastermind himself. Describing the waiting, selection and Do's and Don't's pre-enrollment. All of them were provided with a brief introduction to life at the institute.

CADS was picturing the signboard and the pages of the handbook in his mind.

It read...

Dear Newcomers,

You are about to commence an incredible journey. You all have crossed hurdles of inappropriate codes and incompatible combinations to finally reach here. This is AppSpace which is a bridge between your creator and us. Though there is some waiting till the enrollment starts, it will help you develop strength and endurance to achieve your goal. The time here will seem long and tough, but believe me, all that you undergo here will vanish away as soon as we pick you up.

You just have to follow a basic self-discipline and stick to the rules to be able to cope better with the AppSpace.

Talk to your fellow mates, have healthy inputs, exercise your codes, watch some movies and enjoy your stay here! Confine to your predefined position and avoid strolling through the streets, as you might be lost.

PickApp will bring you to the IOA on the big day.

See you all soon!

Mastermind

CADS's visual thoughts were interrupted by the buzz of the PickApp.

The multicolored app looked like a solar system in itself, loaded with newcomers and was picking up all on the streets of the AppSpace. All apps were jumping queues to enter PickApp at the earliest. They all were served a Welcome code to re-energize themselves and asked to take their orbital space surrounding the instructor at the center.

"Hey, OKAS, it looks like we are electrons in this orbit and she is the nucleus!" exclaimed CADS.

Everyone started looking towards him when OKAS gestured to him to keep quiet.

"Hello and welcome aboard! I am Nucleus of the PickApp and we are travelling to the IOA. Keep your codes fastened for safety as we teleport to the destination. Please let me know if you have any questions."

CADS was excited and was looking outside as they entered the halo and travelled through the beautiful shiny space reaching the IOA.

"I was wondering how they get paid?" Murmured GEK.

"I think it is in virtual coins," said VAD.

"I should have guessed that," said GEK.

"Maybe they don't get enough here in App World as compared to the ones in the human world, that's why they have started these side businesses," said FUNG, overhearing the conversation.

"Nothing bad in having something extra for a rainy day," commented LOI.

"But we didn't carry any virtual coins, how they earned from us in the playzone and the filmzone?" wondered TIB.

"It gets paid by our creator dear. They have to bear these expenses. Afterall, we are their babies," chuckled DOMA.

"Is it? We could have enjoyed some more then. I thought they would ask for payment once we enter the institute, and I thought I would say please deduct from my first earning after I reach the human world" said RISU.

All laughed at his comment.

"Nothing like freebies!" all giggled.

Immersed in the talks, they didn't realize they were almost there. They all were awestruck seeing the majestic Institute of Appology. They were murmuring amongst themselves about how lucky they all are to have made it finally.

Namaste was greeting all the newbies fondly and showing them the way inside. All the movements were recorded as a standard procedure by the Recorder app. As soon as they took their first step, the Recorder app took a photograph which was embedded in the identity card mentioning their initial name, configuration and the creator's name. Was this first step also a giant leap for mankind?

"So did you see anyone actually buying the Energy Codes? Or getting a backdoor entry?" CADS was curious.

"Shhh..." OKAS said and told him to be quiet.

The hall was buzzing with chattering and muttering which transformed into abrupt silence as Mastermind professed the new genre.

"Dear future apps, hope you all are excited about this joyous occasion! I, on behalf of the IOA, proudly officially welcome you all! We are thrilled to welcome you to our esteemed institution as you embark on a remarkable journey of knowledge and growth. Today, we gather here to celebrate the launch of your academic endeavours and to mark the beginning of an exciting chapter in your life. This momentous occasion calls for a grand celebration, filled with joy and enthusiasm and anticipation of the extraordinary achievements and discoveries that lie ahead. As you step into our halls, know that you are not only joining a community of learners but also becoming a part of a legacy of excellence and innovation. Our dedicated faculty and mentors are committed to nursing your talent, inspiring your mind and fostering an environment where you can thrive and reach your fullest potential. Together we will explore new horizons, challenge conventional thinking and create a future that is brighter and more promising. Today, as we witness the launch of your educational journey, we encourage you to embrace every opportunity, overcome obstacles with resilience and embrace the power of collaboration.. Remember, knowledge is the key to unlocking the doors of success, and here you will find all the tools and support you need to unlock these doors.

So, let us raise our voices in celebration, applauding the beginning of an incredible adventure."

Applause and cheering from the crowd of baby apps and all the audience.

"There is a slight change in the program though. The alumni from the institute will be your mentors with whom you can learn one-to-one from now on. I thought of this method to improve the quality as well as to widen our prospects. We are looking for curiosity, determination, unwavering passion for learning in all of you. Together, let us make this an unforgettable experience, propelling us towards a future filled with endless possibilities. Welcome to our community of scholars, visionaries and changemakers!"

Applause and cheering from the crowd of baby apps and all the audience.

OKAS and CADS looked at each other.

"Alumni as mentors? Vow, that sounds awesome!" CADS was elated.

"We need to decide which mentor to choose apart from choosing the stream. It seems like more work to me."

There was noise in the audience as they talked to each other. Their chit-chat was silenced by the Counsellor who took up the microphone to address the crowd. In the meanwhile, Mastermind was scrolling through the messages in the Feedback App.

"Dear all, let's commence the process then."

She gazed across the hall and continued....

"You will be meeting our eminent faculty now, who will train you in the basics to strengthen your foundation. This constitutes an important part in your overall development. As you all come as a product of one or few creators, you have seen a very small part of the human world. This will also give you an insight about various fields which you will need to function well on the other side when you get there. The faculty will now join me on the dais and I will instruct you about when your sessions will start."

"Let me welcome on stage 'The Basic Sciences Department' constituted by experimental geniuses Mr Organ Cell, Ms Chemical Reaction and Mr Velocity Vector." The trio was greeted with applause and cheering. Please welcome our problem solvers 'The Calculations Department' with Mr XY Algebra, Mr Quarter Fractions, Ms Derive Calculus, Ms Plane Geometry, Mr Median Statistics and Ms Random Probability. And next up is our brainy thinkers 'Logic and Reasoning Department', with Mr Deduction and Ms Analysis. Also we have for you, our extensive and submersive 'The Department of Human Psychology' with Mr Conscious Mind and Ms Deep Cognition."

"After you all complete the basic course, you will be choosing your stream of operations and meeting your mentors. But for now, we want you to relax a bit before your sessions start. Mentor choosing is a very different process so I will brief you about that separately after your course completion. Environ will take you to the App rooms, which are specially designed for you to rest, so that you can be fresh for the classes."

All appeared ready to take a nap and relax as they reached their Approoms.

Feedback had a flood of messages and they popped up one by one. Of course it maintained anonymity to allow the weirdest of thoughts to be sent.

"Hi Mastermind, I have to get back to work soon, can we work from home, as in we leave after the meet and continue mentoring from home?"

"I think it's a great idea to do this, but we are not into teaching per se, how will we guide them?"

"When the traditional teaching method could produce apps like us, what is the need for this change and one-on-one program?"

"Can we get something like a guide or tips for mentoring?"

"How will we decide whether the idea they are putting up is worth it? I think it should be voted on or discussed rather than relying on one mentor's opinion."

"What do we do if we feel that the candidate is not fit for the aura he or she chooses?"

"What if two candidates want the same mentor?"

"Should we conduct a kind of exit test to certify or they directly go into the market?"

"If I fall sick during mentoring, does the project gets stalled or delayed, or I get a replacement?"

"Do they submit a thesis during the graduation?"

"How will I be paid for this extra service?"

Mastermind had a strange smile while reading these, but he knew how to handle these.

Approom was where comfort meets luxury. A cozy bed, a work desk, a code-closet, a minibar and attached cleanup space was what all needed. The corridor seemed unending with approoms designed on either side and it intersected at few places too. Similar was the design of the senior wing where the grown up apps were staying; just a few intersections across. The exhausted baby apps decided to crash on the bed before thinking of exploring the new space.

The bell installed in each approom rang and blinked light to signal and wake the babies up for the course. As all came out and met in the corridor, it appeared enlivened. They all were guided to the academic halls by Environ. They didn't realize that they had to attend long hours of theory followed by practical lessons, and do assignments which would eat up all their energy.

The enormous academic hall was different from the classrooms in the human world. While the humans are used to sitting on benches arranged on the ground surface with increasing ground height as you move to backbenchers, here all were in a single vertical plane. It was just like sitting on a small desk hung on the wall, so that all could see the teachers and vice versa. The first class was scheduled to start and all were ready to memorize the excerpts.

Mr Organ Cell was the one to start first. His impressive persona extruded his attractive biology. Dressed in a black slim fit blazer suit and a maroon tie and pocket square, he announced a formal tone to his overall appearance.

After a formal introduction with the class students, he began with a description of animal and plant cell structure. He went on to describe mitosis and meiosis or in simpler terms, the cell division before talking about human chromosomal structure and the DNA helix. In very simple terms, he was able to make them understand the Mendelian inheritance and the gene expression. All of them were immersed in the beauty of the microscopic structures as Mr Cell showed them the microscope and called them to experience it during the practical part of the subject. They also enjoyed the functional models of the organ systems, especially a beating heart. The most difficult part was dissection and all of them expressed disinterest in doing so. Mr Cell explained that it is only a virtual dissection without blood being shed, which made them slightly comfortable in doing it, but couldn't prevent DOMA and TIBS to collapse seeing all the inside of humans. They were awakened by the professor as he told everyone it is a common phenomenon to faint seeing something unpleasant as this.

Though all the babies were trying to retain every information coming their way, they were unsure as to how this would be helpful in their future applications.

"Does this human heart work throughout day and night in the human world professor? Doesn't it need rest?" asked FUNG.

"If it rests, how do you think that person will survive?" laughed Mr Cell and continued, *"All the organs have specific functions and they have to do it for the human to survive and lead a healthy life."*

"I had a very detailed study of DNA analysis with my creator, professor. It was complicated yet interesting how it is different in all of them," expressed ZAD.

"You are right ZAD, but same is with you all. Your code arrangements are unique, and that makes you special. It is your identity and can be tested the same way as DNA analysis."

"Vow, that's amazing," said MART.

"I always feel their brain is so complex," said OKAS.

"Yes OKAS, the whole nervous system is an intricate arrangement to have an appropriate response to the stimulus. But the brain, I would say, is still too vast to study. It is therefore not a detailed topic in your basic course, although other organ systems are."

As the class came to an end, they felt they were adept in basic biology. The break between two classes was the same as in the human world. A lot of chatting and muttering and complete silence the moment the teacher arrives.

Ms Chemical Reaction was the next to introduce them to inorganic and organic chemistry. She looked stunning in a long red dress, a knit hat and a black coat. She took an attendance and then commenced. She introduced them to the concepts of elements and compounds and the atomic table. Baby apps were excited to know about exothermic and endothermic reactions and were amused to see colourful compounds and fumes coming out of the flasks and test tubes as Ms Reaction explained about various chemical reactions. They were happy to hold a large burette and a tiny Durham's tube used for the experiments as she started the practical lessons. VAD almost jumped back when fire came out of HOFA's flask and all smiled looking at each other. Ms Reaction kept calm and extinguished the fire only to make them do the experiment again.

"These chemical reactions are so interesting, but I feel scared seeing VAD," said BUJI.

"I understand. But there is no harm if you study the instructions carefully and then perform," smiled Ms Reaction, then turning to WIVA and UPO, *"I hope you are enjoying the experiment."*

"Yes professor, I am very excited. But we were just curious to know about the radioactivity," said UPO, *"its exposure has had an impact on my creator's life."*

"See UPO, it is a property exhibited by certain types of matter emitting energy and subatomic particles spontaneously. In other words, the spontaneous disintegration of unstable atomic nuclei to to form more energetically stable atomic nuclei. They are especially harmful to humans if there is exposure. That's why they have to be contained and disposed of in very strict conditions. I can give you a special reading material about it. We can talk about it more if you have any doubts."

"I wanted to know about the excimer, professor," said WIVA, *"some kind of laser in the human world, my creator underwent some treatment with it."*

"It is a shortened form of excited dimer, a complex formed between two fluorophore molecules of the same type—one in the excited state and the other in the ground state. This laser is used in eye surgeries, skin treatments etc. They are pulsed lasers that emit UV light."

"Can there be a quadrimer too then, professor?" wondered EJA.

"Technically there can be, in fact we developed large nthmer with uncountable excited molecules in our lab here and it is quite powerful."

They all were very impressed to know about so many things from Ms Reaction that they didn't realize it was almost the end of her class.

They were told that the next class will be taken by Mr Velocity Vector and they need to be patient as he walks very slowly and will take a few moments to arrive.

"How come one walks slowly when the name is velocity?" Asked GEK.

"Maybe his vector is in some other direction," commented RISU.

They giggled as he entered the hall. A slender built and kyphotic back with simple white clothing and flat slippers made the genius teacher look undernourished, weak and fragile. This totally contrasted when he spoke in a firm and authoritative voice. The simple topics of light, sound, matter, energy and force to complex principles of magnetism, gravity, quantum mechanics and astronomy seemed to be incorporated in their thought processes as he continued his lectures.

"I didn't understand this concept of dimensions, professor," said XAB.

"It is very exciting XAB. Humans started with three dimensions of space, that is length, width and height. Then addition of time made 4 dimensions which are acceptable as of now. Although according to their string theory based on octonionic matrices, there can be upto 26 dimensions. They are still unaware that there are more to be discovered, we are in nth dimension, the dimension where counting ends, so you can well imagine how this universe works."

"And that humans are way behind us, though they created us initially," said LOI.

"That is the power of transformation everyone has once he decides to do so," says Mr Vector.

The most interesting aspect for all was the expanding universe, the Big bang theory and the concept of quantum foam. OKAS was enjoying this class the most and also missing his creator, SJ. They were indulged in his epic description of the place App World is. He told them, the humans don't know that we all are in this nth dimension which they call a black hole as they can't conceptualize anything further. This is in GAIA BH1 in Ophiuchus constellation as called by humans. We are in this one of the so called black holes closest to the human world on Earth; that's why our universe is Earthverse.

"Does it mean there are other such universes as well, professor?" asked SIL.

"Definitely there are. But we are still trying to find signs of App life there. We haven't found App traces anywhere else. We are the only ones developing apps."

"What about the closest neighbour GAIA BH2 in the Centaurus constellation, professor?" asked OKAS, *"I heard about it from my creator."*

"Your creator is a great physicist. But as I said before, there have been no signs of App life anywhere. In other words, GAIA BH2 is also a neighbour, and we haven't observed any activity there yet."

"So if we don't have any other questions, I think we have completed most of the things, and I will meet you virtually later, in case you have doubts in your assignments," said Mr Vector rushing his way out, albeit in his own speed.

"Maybe we have some brothers or sisters in GAIA BH2," laughed AVA, *"your question freaked the professor out OKAS!"*

"I think so too, maybe he saw something creepy while focusing his scope" said CADS.

"I heard assignments, and that freaks me out," said OKAS, *"this one I might be okay but not the previous two subjects."*

"I am also thinking about the assignments aspect," said KOI.

"And I am thinking, is this going to continue or we get some break?" said a tired PIDS.

"This is for our own future PIDS, be serious and committed," encouraged VAD.

They were told they had some time to go to App rooms to take rest and finish assignments, and also to connect to the teachers in case of difficulties, and that they have to reassemble for next sessions when the bell rings.

The assignments were monotonous, lengthy and tricky. Answering popping questions on the screen and practically performing virtual dissection and labeling, doing experiments as the virtual chemicals popped out of screen, problem solving in physics. The teachers were available to solve silliest of questions. They had some energy drinks and relaxation but there was no time for socializing. They all wanted some rest before the next classes.

The bell rang again. Of course, it had to. Only poor baby apps didn't want it to! They came together in the corridor and were taken to the academic hall.

They talked on the way about their experiences with the assignments. Most of them seemed confident in the basic sciences and were ready to take on the next challenge- Mathematics.

"So many teachers for a single subject?" asked AVA.

"It is so complicated and vast," said GEK, *"maybe that's why."*

"But so are all the subjects," commented CADS.

"Let's see what they have for us," said VAD.

"Shhhh..." said FUNG as he saw the teacher coming.

The sessions started with the anxiety-inducing algebra with finding value of variables in different types of equations once you are given with constants and was full of formulae you need to understand and use at proper places. Mr XY Algebra was a funny teacher who introduced humor in the classroom and made everyone feel at ease. He usually preferred to dress casually and also took things the same way. The babies liked his way of teaching when he explained the concepts with real life examples. Be it a linear equation compared to finding speed and distance or quadratic equations compared to the parabolic curve like in movement of objects when thrown off the ground, he told everything in simpler form which was easy to grasp and relatable. The concept of variable which keeps changing made most of them love the subject.

"Professor, I understand that the two variables will be interrelated and will keep changing values against a constant, but can the constant become a variable in changing dimensions?" asked OKAS.

"See, it hasn't been observed till now and humans as well as ourselves couldn't prove that constants have changed. But it doesn't mean that it can't happen. We still have to witness that."

OKAS was slightly convinced but left intrigued at the possibility. All others were looking at him thinking which world he is from to be asking such weird questions. As OKAS was lost in his thoughts, The next class had almost begun.

Mr Quarter Fractions looked full and complete while everyone wondered he might just be a quarter. Hidden behind his large spectacles, his eyes were sharp to observe a lost OKAS. He reached out to him quickly and patted him to wake him up. His nicely parted hair and ironed clothes spoke of his love for grooming himself well. He started his class with simple fractions and moved on to real numbers, imaginary numbers, rational and irrational numbers and complex numbers. Though everyone retained interest and understood things well, they began to feel restless when he started with continued fractions and the convergence rate of partial convergents.

"Are these going to help us in any way Professor?" asked VAD.

"Yes, because this thing is literally going beyond my scope of thinking and understanding," said LOI.

"Well, they all are interesting concepts and will definitely be useful to you in coming future especially if you choose finance and computing but yes, otherwise you might not be dealing with much of it," said Mr Fractions.

"We didn't want to offend you Professor, It's just that we don't understand them very well," said AVA.

"No problem at all, I understand. It is indeed a very challenging part of mathematics. Maybe I went slightly deeper in the subject, towards the things you need not know at this level. You can always come back to me in case you need help," said Mr Fractions as he left the class.

Ms Derive Calculus was quick to enter as soon as Mr Fractions left. Hair tightly tied back to expose a large forehead, a pair of focused eyes and unwithering stare could make anyone nervous. She covered herself in a large black cloak and moved constantly as she spoke.

"So you all are here to know the basics of Calculus. It is the study of continuous change," she started, *"but let me remind you, it is not as easy as you think. You can stop me in between, ask questions, but most importantly be attentive and try to grasp even the minutest detail."*

All felt even more nervous now. They were thinking how teachers differ from each other. While some are so friendly, some are so strict sounding. The commonality being they all are trying to make us understand the basics.

They all listened to her as she explained about limits, differential calculus, integral calculus and functional theory. *"Its use is not limited to mathematics. Rather you think of anything important, calculus is a part of it. You cannot escape it. Be it structural engineering, be it space exploration, be it stock markets or be it blood pressure and heart rate graph, it is used everywhere. I will give you a few assignments, which will make your concepts better. You can always ask me if you have problems."*

They were excited to learn about calculus, but were confused whether they understood everything. While they were still deriving at what level they were, the next class was about to start.

Ms Plane Geometry was short and sweet with a pleasant smile on her face. Her subject was Geometry, but she told that she would be teaching trigonometry too as the faculty for trigonometry were not available.

She made them imagine and live the various shapes and taught them calculations of their area, volume and complex parameters. It sounded very artistic and full of fun. They felt confident early on in the basic concepts but needed some practice to master drawing various structures. The hard part was trigonometry where they needed to find values of sine, cosine, tangent, cotangent, secant and cosecant of multiple angles. They understood its importance to find heights and distances in aviation, navigation and engineering, but it was seemingly difficult.

"Professor, Geometry is fine with me, but I can't get heads and tails of trigonometry," said FUNG.

"Me too, professor," said RISU.

"Me too," shouted all.

"It's okay to feel that way," said Ms Geometry, *"it appears tough at first, but then becomes simpler as you go further."*

"Why did the trigonometry faculty not come to teach themselves?" asked BUJI.

"They went away unannounced actually, and that has happened for the first time in the history of IOA, that's why I had to teach you."

"I wonder if this boring and complex trigonometry is the reason the faculty ran away," commented HOFA, laughing.

"Maybe!" said Ms Geometry, laughing.

Her class was light and it seemed to end quite soon. They wished it could continue for some more time as they didn't know how the next teacher was going to be.

Mr Median Statistics was already there to start his class. Dressed in a white suit, tie and hat with a big white mustache, he entered with a walking stick and appeared arrogant in his demeanor as he asked all the students to stop talking. He started by giving problem questions and asked them to find mean, median and mode. Only OKAS could do it. And then he started with his explanation of all these and about the normal distribution, standard deviation and confidence interval. He told them that statistics forms a very important part in every field especially involving research.

"Do you know you can apply statistical tests to establish a cause and effect relationship and to rule it out as well?" he continued, *"Even if you want to find your own performance over years or your revenue, statistics will give you the answers."*

The class was important but dry. All understood the basics well to be able to use it in future.

Last class before break was about to begin. Ms Random Probability elegantly entered the classroom with a dress full of random colors and a vibrant smile. She spoke of randomness, chance and errors of prediction. She elaborated that probability was a very ancient known thing to humans, but it developed as a branch of mathematics and added value to medicine, law, philosophy and even fortune telling. All were amused listening to this interesting theory and wanted to actually try solving problems. This was the first subject which they were wanting to do the assignments.

"What is the probability that I will graduate, professor?" asked AVA, laughing.

"The same as mine," commented CADS, smiling.

They were jokingly wanting to explore probability in common scenarios, thoroughly enjoying the class and didn't come to know when it ended. It was time for another break after which the final stack of lessons were scheduled. They were more used to the assignments and could finish them quickly to meet up with one another in the corridor and gather in one approom to gossip and talk.

"All our teachers put so much effort into teaching us, I wonder don't they get bored and want to go to the human world for a change?" started VAD.

"Yes, that's why we should respect them, they are working tirelessly without money or fame to develop us," said BUJI.

"I wonder what they are actually?" asked OKAS.

"What do you mean?" asked GEK.

"I mean, we were picked up by PickApp, greeted by Namaste app, recorded by Recorder app, transported by Environ app, guided by Counsellor app; but these teachers are not apps, they develop apps like us. Even Mastermind, I think is not an app. So what are they?" elaborated OKAS.

"That's an interesting observation, OKAS. I think we can ask them directly tomorrow," said UPO.

"Yes, I thought so too," said OKAS.

"One more addition to your question would be, where did they come from? Like we know we came from the human world and wish to go back there, while some of us might like the place too much to just stay here, like

PickApp, Environ, Namaste, Recorder, Counsellor. But where are they from and how did they come to App World at all?" said XAB.

"That makes so much sense," said FUNG.

"I think it doesn't make any sense. I am getting a chill down the spine thinking who these all are?" said DOMA.

"It sounds creepy," said HOFA.

"I think we all should just focus on finishing the course and start with mentors, this will just give nightmares," said an upset EJA.

"She is right," said KOI, *"let's go back and take some rest."* All of them looked at each other and then got up to go, still thinking about the discussion. OKAS was the most perturbed and could not get much rest. The bell rang again.

Environ was there to guide them to the academic hall. On the way, OKAS managed to gather some courage and ask him, *"What are the teachers here, Mr Environ?"*

"What do you intend to ask?" said Environ.

"I mean they are not apps like us, so what are they and how did they come to App World?"

"Even I don't know OKAS, as I also came here as a student and later took up a job here itself. I never thought about it. But it is definitely something we can ask them or the Mastermind." They had reached the academic hall and taken their seats. Mr Deduction and Ms Analysis were going to deliver a joint session.

"The art of step by step analysis and deduction of correct information is what this class is all about," started Mr Deduction. *"And logical reasoning to emanate all doubts and prove your point is the goal,"* continued Ms Analysis.

"And it requires only two things- focus and common sense!" laughed Mr Deduction.

"Which is quite uncommon with humans," said Ms Analysis.

"So, there is lot of assumption, probability of more than one solution and changing perspective. What may sound apt to you, may sound illogical to others and vice versa," said Mr Deduction.

"Basically we examine evidence, identify patterns and draw logical conclusions. Now suppose a family consists of six members A, B, C, D, E and F. B is the son of C but C is not mother of B. A and C are a married couple. E is the brother of C. D is the daughter of A. F is the brother of A. How many children does A have?" asked Ms Analysis.

All went into deep thinking to deduce the solution.

"I think two, B and D," answered LOI.

"That was quick and correct," said Ms Analysis, *"can you share with everyone how you reached this conclusion?"*

"You told B is the son of C but C is not the mother of B so I assumed he is the father of B. As A and C are married couple and F and E are brothers of A and C respectively, they can't be A's children. D is clearly daughter of A. So I deduced that B and D are son and daughter of A and C," LOI confidently explained.

"Wonderful!" exclaimed Mr Deduction, *"Similarly, if I say If it is light outside, it is daytime. It is light outside, then what is your conclusion?"*

"That it is daytime, I suppose," said AVA.

"Exactly!" said Mr Deduction, *"the only thing I will change in your answer is that you didn't suppose, you deduced."*

"See it sounds so easy, you just have to reach to a sensible conclusion based on presented information," said Ms Analysis, *"we will give you lot of such questions to practice and let us know how you feel."*

"Is that all?" they asked themselves as two of them left the class.

Psychology was the next in line for the classes. Mr Conscious Mind and Ms Deep Cognition were there for the joint session.

"What is mind? The mind is composed of inner structures that organise information from the environment, connect this information with prior stored knowledge, and process information and knowledge to

form a decision upon which to act." started Mr Mind. *"We need to know about it in detail as all of us are going to affect human psychology in one or the other way."*

"As Mr Mind mentioned, our subject is all about what is going on up there. It involves gaining knowledge, comprehension, thinking, reasoning, perception, judgement, memory and problem solving," continued Ms Cognition.

"We will not go into anatomical details of the nervous system as it will be too complex but we would like to tell you a broader perspective. Though philosophy has an important part in advent of psychology and it was called rationalism by Plato, involving basic principles understood by rational thought to create knowledge by humans themselves, the later philosophers believed in empiricism, meaning the knowledge was gained more through observation of world around people," explained Mr Mind.

"Rightly said so, now it is mainly cognitive psychology we focus on. It is basically processing of sensory inputs leading to the final result that is learning, understanding, reasoning, behaving, forming memories and making decisions etc.," continued Ms Cognition.

"Will this really help us in future?" asked EJA.

"All of you will interact with humans through their mobile interface. Whether they choose other app over you, how much they are dependent on you, whether they will continue using you; this all is affected by the inputs you will provide to affect their psychology. So when you develop yourself and build on your layers, you have to make sure to strike the right chord. That's why it's important. Else you will be a futile, useless, unwanted app for them," said Mr Mind.

"But we can't judge what they want, can we?" asked TIBS.

"We can study app performances through previous years, their statistics of download numbers, usage, revenue etc. to make smart choices," said Ms Cognition, *"indirectly knowing the psyche."*

"How about we do that in our assignments so that can help us in choosing our streams too?" asked KOI.

"That's a wonderful idea!" said Mr Mind.

"We will guide you through it," added Ms Cognition.

This marked the end of the basic lessons as the baby apps retired to the app rooms. After finishing the assignments, the selection process was going to begin. Presumably fun to choose mentors, and having one-on-one supervised development was a dream going to be true. OKAS was still thinking about the nature of faculty and was restless. Going back and forth in the corridor about is it the real app development process conceived by creators, made him confused. Without any rest, he was feeling exhausted and realized that it was already time for the next step.

Timezone 3: The Selection

The Counsellor was as usual dressed in a flowy solid colored gown with a charming smile to welcome the baby apps after successful course completion and was ready to guide them about the next process.

"I want all of you to head towards the atrium, where you will be interacting with your mentors. The path from this hall to the atrium is a specially designed one. You choose your stream on the way so that you enter the correct 'aura' (Aura is like a cubicle and is a dead end to the path of the stream chosen). You will then have a choice of the mentor from your selected stream. You can talk to them through the Mentor app which is an interface between you and your mentor. You just have to enter your IOA ID number, which will be provided to you as you start moving on the path.

All were listening to her attentively.

"It is of utmost importance that you don't discuss amongst yourselves, as it has to be solely your decision of what you want to be."

Nervous, CADS was looking at OKAS.

"And now, the most important part. About the 'aura switching' and 'multi aura certification'. Earlier, we allowed three switches, in case you are not comfortable with your selected stream. From now on, it has been changed to unlimited switches, till you find the stream of your choice. This is because we don't want you to linger on with something you don't like. There can be an unusual situation where you are not comfortable with any of the streams you choose and you reach the end of choices. That would mean that you are not someone who can go along with the existing streams. In that case, you are automatically diverted to the research wing headed by our mastermind. Another possible situation would be where you like a stream but you want to explore other streams as well. This also has been well thought of, and it would require you to complete certain time zones in a particular aura to get certified and then move to the next aura. If you are able to finish the required time zones in the next aura as well, you will be certified accordingly and will be able to work across the streams.

The order in which you will stand in the queue is based on your scores. It includes your creator's app history, their standing in the society, their App intent, their resources to their previous App performance and revenue, apart from your assignment scores in the basic course subjects. We have given appropriate weightage to all the elements and made your final score. The ones with higher score get to select the stream first."

It was too much of an information overload but the baby apps were trying their best to imbibe and process the details so that they can have a seamless experience to final certification.

As the baby apps made a queue and walked towards the path many of them were discussing amongst themselves about which would be a good stream to go in and also trying to fathom the degree of anxiety they were having.

The path leading to the various Auras was extraordinary. The virtual wall enclosing the space was displaying all the graduates of the Institute of Appology presenting their experiences at the institute and their life thereafter. It seemed to update every single time zone to give the latest information about what is happening to the alumni in the real world. All of them were trying to attract more and more baby apps to join their aura so that they have a strong hold and position in the human world.

Mastermind had gone through the messages on the Feedback app, and had made arrangements to take care of everyone's concerns.

OKAS and CADS were walking slowly alongwith the fellowmates. CADS stepped in first and was given his identity card as he entered the atrium. OKAS was the next to go in following CADS.

The enormous atrium was enlivened by the presence of star apps. The baby apps were star struck seeing the alumni behind the interface.

As CADS chose to go to the entertainment aura, he looked back at OKAS for a secret affirmation. OKAS nodded giving his silent reply to CADS's unasked question. CADS chose Noflix as his mentor. As he approached the interface and entered his ID number to login, Noflix logged in from the other side and both of them could see each other. CADS felt so miniscule as compared to the famous Noflix.

"Hi CADS! Hope you are feeling well. Thanks for choosing me as your mentor." Noflix started the conversation.

"Hello Mr. Noflix, how are you? So nice to finally meet you! You are my inspiration and I have always wanted to become like you." CADS expressed his admiration for Noflix.

All other fellowmates were also choosing their streams and CADS saw AVA choose entertainment as well as she entered his aura and walked to Hotshot.

OKAS was still befuddled which stream to choose when he saw the abstruse auras in front of him.

OKAS remembered SJ, his creator. A well read and learned physicist and philosopher who wanted to develop an app to help human beings overcome their day to day struggles and hardships. OKAS had soaked in all the knowledge SJ had transferred to him. But he was muddled about which stream would be best to achieve what SJ desired. SJ had once told him, you are my brainchild, and you have to be a step ahead in taking the right decision to help humanity. He knew SJ would be waiting eagerly in the human world to welcome his best version.

Still trying to decide, OKAS moved to a side as his fellowmates were in a hurry to move to the auras.

SIL had decided to go to Qwitter. Few were going to the Gs, as MART chose M and ZAD chose G. XAB chose to go to WeTube.

OKAS saw GEK moving to FaceLook and HOFA moving to WhatsUp. All the big names were being chosen fast and OKAS was still muddled.

BUJI wanted to go to Timber but as DOMA already went ahead of her, BUJI quickly stepped forward to request DOMA if she could choose someone else. DOMA decided on the spot to go to Anagram.. Minetough was always FUNG's first choice as was Rolox for TIB.

PIDS seemed lost but finally found a way to Andry Buds and RISU moved to Sandy Rush happily. LOI found his inspiration in Fred Fyre as he was seen moving jerkily to his aura. The spots were getting filled faster than imagination and everyone appeared focused and determined about their choices.

OKAS's predicament made his chances of selecting big names dismal. WIVA walked confidently to Emay and UPO chose Amadon while there were many in a bunch choosing the other apps in the shopping aura. EJA had made her mind to go to Disey and KOI had a liking for Prim.

VAD always wanted to be the master of money, and that's what he chose. He walked quietly to the finance and banking aura. As the toppers had taken all the cream, the fellowmates in the queue started moving to not-so-big names. OKAS was wondering, is he the only one with a mindblock?

All the baby apps were chatting with their mentors and were overwhelmed with the whole experience.

The auras witnessed the most awaited part of this new beginning- the interaction.

As CADS continued his chat with Noflix, all other baby apps had also started their conversation.

AVA was with Hotshot.

"Ms Hotshot, how did you choose entertainment aura?"

"Dear, just call me Hotshot! I always wanted to entertain. As you know I started with sports though, more so cricket, but later with Disey, I became a total entertainment package."

"It might sound silly, but how do you conceive and have babies? Isn't it a human thing?"

Laughing, *"It is not at all about the pregnancy where the baby is in the womb and the tummy grows bigger. But yes, the bonding and attachment is the same. The way babies carry their parent's genes, our babies carry few of our codes."*

"I get it now. But is the whole thing difficult for female apps, as in the human world? Like taking care of kids, attending to work, maintaining relationships?"

"I would not say it is easy. But as humans we also balance everything well, especially if you have support from your partner. Our babies are all fully developed beings as such, they just need a bit of grooming. If in case they land up in any trouble, we have rectification support. Only issue is, if they don't do well in this competitive world, it is painful to see them drown in depression and negative thoughts. We are lucky to have DoctorApp to treat all of us. You are too small to think about all this, you should focus on your graduation for now."

"Well, how do you suggest I start my journey?"

"AVA, you are brilliant. I would advise you to think of something different you would want to develop in the entertainment sector, something which you or your creator might have discussed or dreamt of. Because I believe, to succeed, you should either do something new or something different."

"I actually thought of taking entertainment to the next level."

"What do you have in mind?"

"The characters and the environment in our shows and movies can come to life."

"Tell me more."

"I was thinking, the way a person wears a VR device and feels to be at a particular place and feels it is real; albeit with eyes into the device, how about giving that environment there and then with eyes open."

"How do you plan to do it?"

"Aerial conglomeration of codes and creation of virtual reality ."

"It is difficult to accomplish, don't you think?"

"My creator is the one who developed Environ app. But Mastermind gave him a job at institute, he could never make to the human world. He gives you the environment needed instantly, I want to stack it with options for individual needs."

"You mean to say if a boy is sitting in his living room in NewYork, and he logs in to you, tells you he wants to enjoy African safari, you can create it in his living room?"

"Yes, it is possible. And even something from the past, if someone is watching the iconic Michel Jackson performing on stage, and wants to dance with him, it's possible. I have seen all codes of Environ, all I need to do is develop few more to work correctly with your guidance."

Hotshot is picturing as AVA is speaking. *"You have all my support AVA, let's do this!"*

HOFA is with WhatsUp..

"Hi Ms Whatsup, so nice to see you! You are a big success today! How did this platform occur to you?"

"My creators BA and JK were actually with Kahoo for very long. And you must be aware that Kahoo had a messenger service way back in the 90s era. They wanted me to be every person's messenger, and here I am!"

"You are superb! Especially after introducing your voice messaging, editable messaging, disappearing messages, you have tapped the human requirements like no one else! That's why I wanted you to be my mentor."

"Thanks for such kind words HOFA. I know you are the creation of one of the most successful minds."

"The whole experience here is so overwhelming!"

"Yes, I agree. First time you step out of your home to the institute, the mixed feelings of determination to fulfill ambitions, future insecurity, homesickness, anxiety in a whole new place with all new people makes you really uncomfortable. But slowly, you adjust."

"Your words acted like magic meditation for me! I hope I can start right away."

"Sure HOFA, tell me what have you planned?"

"I wanted the messaging and conversation to be in real time."

"In Real time? You mean like the audio and video call feature? But that's already there."

"No, I mean once someone logs into me, and sends a message, the other person hears it as if the sender is standing in front of him and speaking to him; like told on a video call, but this one is without even seeing the device The person just appears virtually."

"Okay, so you want to upgrade the messaging platform to be like a video message sent every time a sender sends a text message. But then, the humans can already record a video message and send it."

"This is different from that, Ms WhatsUp. This is what I call adhesion. This is like me sending a text when the person cannot or doesn't want to show the face or voice to the other, but this will show them live with their emotions and feelings at the time they are texting."

"I understand the adhesion phenomenon you detailed, but still I am not sure whether it will click with humans. As many of them actually want to hide behind the messages. But if you want to pursue this, we can move forward."

"I have given it a thought, and I want to do it this way. If you feel along the process, that it is really not going to work, then I will ponder over it and start afresh."

"That sounds like a plan to me. Only suggestion is to have a Plan B ready in case it doesn't work; that will save your time."

"Sure, I will do that."

SIL is with Qwitter.

"Ms Qwitter, you are so popular and yet maintain a bubbly and chirpy persona on one hand and so much calm and poise on the other, how do you maintain this balance?"

"Balance is all in the mind SIL. I learnt it from JD, my creator."

"JD alongwith NG,BS,EW right?"

"Correct, My life is like an open book. Amidst all the stormy legal issues, acquisition, rebranding, I still stand firm because of the balance. JD used to say you are like short burst of inconsequential information, like the chirp of a bird. That's why I used to look like a bird before."

"But little did he know, the inconsequential words had to have consequences, I guess."

"Oh if only we knew what was coming. Still unsure whether I was microblogging or social networking, I didn't know during my days at Oteo that I will become so popular. But fame has it's own drawbacks. See the way I have been dragged into controversies of homophobia and anti semitism and targeted on various occasions for hate speech and disinformation."

"You have been misunderstood many times."

"Yes SIL, if I could make everything alright, that is what would give me some peace. But I am really sorry I got carried away with my own story. We are here to focus on your future. What do you think is apt for you?"

"This is what I thought could be helpful."

"What?"

"Making things alright."

"Cleaning up Qwitter err X."

"I want to be a cleaning mop for hate, misunderstanding and rumors."

"But how is it possible?"

"Close monitoring and warning of modification of qweet nanoseconds before the senders click 'post', 'reqweet' or 'quote reqweet'.."

"But isn't that not taking away freedom of speech? You will be in legal trouble."

"You know better than me that trouble is inevitable and unavoidable because of some elements which have the sole motive of propagating such things. But we can atleast try from our end to make things alright."

"I couldn't agree more. But have you thought about the ways to do it?"

"X-Clean: that is the name I thought for myself (chuckles). A highly complex code to monitor a qweet while it is being written by the user, and sending warning in a flash to reconsider; if they don't reconsider, it goes to autodelete or automodify by me. How does it sound?"

"It sounds superb in a perfect world. But this will be considered dictatorship, taking away freedom of speech and we will lose our user base as well."

"Then what should I do?"

"I think you limit it to warning, and name it 'red qweet' once posted, segregating it as inappropriate or misleading. You can always clean up after they are posted, the autodelete option for sensitive content. This way we will avoid legal trouble as well as preserve our users."

"And I will cleanup all your worrisome past, is that okay?"

"It is the best I can think of! You are a gem. Thanks for being such a pious being. You should not be X-Clean, you should be X-Pure or maybe just Pure, as you can purify other social networking and blogging sites too."

SIL smiles.

GEK is with Facelook.

"Hello Mr Facelook, this is me GEK."

"You can have a seat." Facelook continues with his downward gaze and doesn't look at GEK.

"I wished to learn from you to graduate with honors."

"Graduation with honors doesn't guarantee what they call success GEK, and doesn't guarantee a perfect happy life for sure."

"Then what should be my motto?"

"You aim for achieving excellence in what you do, be passionate about what you do, that gives you contentment. That is the best you can get. Success, failure, happiness, sorrow and many other things are just temporary. What is important is the state of mind, which, if contended, is unbeatable by negativity."

"You have so much depth in your thoughts."

"What I chose to become might seem superficial, but I actually can't stand two-faced beings."

"Mr Facelook I always wanted people to connect on a deeper level rather than just connect for likes, appreciation and living in a self developed unreal world."

"GEK, do you really think it is possible?"

"I feel once they see and feel the beauty of connecting that way, they would come out of this fake world."

"It is difficult to achieve a task."

"We can at least try."

"So how do you want to do this?"

"To get to know the person better based on his profile, posts, their own likes and comments on others profile, their searches and maybe extend to their demeanour on other platforms and suggest match connections."

"This sounds more like matrimony and too much intrusion of privacy."

"Similar, I agree. But don't you think it will provide more meaningful relationships, be it a friend, partner or spouse? As far as intrusion is considered, this is very minute I feel."

"Could be. Let's try this out."

"Not to intrude into your personal space, but I just wanted to know is all well between you and the Gs?"

"No problem, I prefer to talk openly about such things. Professional rivalry is bound to happen when you are competing in the same aura, and that's what happened when I started almost the same timezone as Onput. But Gs realized that I was doing better, so they had to call DoctorApp to provide euthanasia to Onput."

"Is euthanasia legal?"

"It is the decision of creators, app family the app himself. It is not legal for humans, but for us it is. It is also called dissolution of codes.."

"Or they could take that app back to the institute to modify or restructure or reaurate (assigning to different aura)."

"That's a brilliant thought GEK! I will send it as a feedback to Mastermind."

BUJI was with Timber.

"Hi Mx Timber, you look awesome!"

"Great to see you BUJI."

"Same here. I have actually been very indecisive till the end. I never knew what will be the best for me. But then I saw you and realized that there is something more in me which I can explore."

"I appreciate your honesty, especially in choosing me."

"I have been through phases where I felt lonely and misunderstood. You are the best to understand my plight."

"Are you..."

"Yes my creator is a transgender woman and I have seen her crying for inclusion in the society, but has just received hatred, seclusion and disgust from the judgemental society. I transpire her feelings in me."

"I got it. It is a difficult world. Actually when I first came into being, my creators SR, JM and WW never knew my inclination and I faced a lot of legal issues including discrimination against the transgender. That was the time I came out openly and told them to include more gender and sexual orientation options."

"But still the human world is not too comfortable with LGBTQ+."

"It can be a long discussion. But these are out of our reach. It finally comes to what humans want."

"If I say, I want to do something in that regard, do you think it will be a good option for my graduation?"

"For graduation, I would suggest you choose something which will have a wider network and user base, you can always do something once you establish yourself. Otherwise you will be crushed before you can taste fame. People are so obsessed with gender reveal videos and photoshoots to understand the depth of this situation."

"You are right. Then let me go with family empowerment. Because inclusion starts with family. I want to start something like family dating, wherein two or more members take out time to go out to understand each other better. If the communication is strong and the bond is great, there will not be problems of sharing and acceptance."

"People might say we all go out on vacations, what is new about this?"

"That is different, where you actually want to enjoy a destination maybe with a bit of opening up with each other, but it is primarily destination oriented and involves too many people. This is actually a date where you talk about yourself, listen to the other person and grow an intimacy."

"I hope it clicks!"

"I hope so too!"

GEK and BUJI were unaware that they had chosen similar paths, through different mentors.

DOMA was with Anagram.

"Hey, Hi DOMA, come up over here!" Anagram was seated obliquely at an elevated throne like seater and waved at DOMA as she entered the aura.

DOMA looks up *"Hi Ms Anagram!"*

"The angle looks so good for my latest profile picture that I am sitting here."

"I was longing to see you."

"So how come you decided to choose this aura for your graduation?"

"I always wanted to become the center of attraction, very famous and very rich like you!"

"Welcome aboard. Let's expand our business. So what do you have in mind?"

"Only difference is that I wanted all this but without any filters, do you really think it would work?"

"Depends on what you actually have in your mind. Anything done with true passion gives you insta-success!"

"I want the world to see more of the real self. More about body positivity, appreciation of all different body types and redefining the beauty standards."

"It is a tough competition in this glamorized world. I agree that it is all fake but fake is what sells!"

"That is the main reason I want to redefine everything. To prevent the harmful effects of chemicals and cosmetic surgeries to change the appearance on one hand and also the mental health issues involved with exclusion of certain body types and appearances on the other hand. If established celebrities start believing in and accepting their own appearance, all the followers will do the same. I just want everyone to find that they are beautiful and that they are right for their real self."

"It will definitely boost the morale and confidence of everyone, especially the teenagers and youth."

"So does it mean that you approve of my project?"

"I totally agree but with the disclaimer people might not want to see the real self themselves!" (laughs)

"We can officially start it then."

"I don't see why not?"

MART and ZAD went to M and G respectively. The inseparable couple was sitting together to welcome the duo.

"Hello MART and ZAD! Welcome to our aura." G exclaimed.

"Our areas of operation overlap and so we decided to see you together. We can discuss how both of you want to function both independently and in sync." M added.

"My thinking actually was to start the virtual to real mailbox experience." MART expressed.

All look puzzled.

"I mean we send the e-mail which gets delivered in real time to the recipient."

"I don't think it is feasible." M said.

"It is, Mr. M." ZAD continued.

"But for that you need to know the face behind the email address, I mean the physical being." G had a frown while speaking.

"And even if this is possible, is it just for an enhanced joy of reading on paper or something more? As it doesn't make much sense to me." M angrily spoke.

"Mr. M and Ms G, what about having a DNA scanner on my search engine, which loads a person's bio instead of just the IP address?" ZAD looked at everyone while speaking confidently.

"What?" Both M and G shockingly exploded.

"I worked with my creator on a DNA analysis project earlier, and I wanted to utilize the knowledge for improving the search, and what is better than incorporating it with Ms G? It could exactly locate the person behind the keypad or keyboard or voice just by scanning part of the body to get DNA structure on my electronic microscope embedded app, and can direct mails and communications to them, very well physically." ZAD said.

"But that would be illegal." M was taken aback.

"There will be increased cyber security features. It will help reduce fake IDs, lessen void communications and decrease cyber crimes." MART said.

"But it will also make people fear using our search engine and mailing service, which will greatly impact our business, don't you think?" G was angry.

Both MART and ZAD started together *"We don't think people with fake IDs and accounts or people who wish to take undue advantage of existing services are the ones we want to depend on to flaunt our business targets. It should be just for people we care about, the real ones. And they won't mind it at all."*

"But they might have a fear of giving away their personal information to us." G said, normalizing.

"Like illegal immigrants who are otherwise not criminals." M said.

"And an illicit relationship where parenthood could be revealed?" G added.

"But they already committed crime, if you think rationally according to human societal norms. It could become more streamlined and safe this way as the information won't be revealed to us, it will be to the local police authority. It could make the world a better place." Both said.

"We could support this, but still have tons of doubts about how it will be perceived?" Both M and G said looking at each other.

"Let's see."

XAB was with WeTube.

"Hi XAB!"

"Hey Mr. WeTube, how are you?"

"I am good, let's talk briefly about your plan."

"I might not be an all rounder like you, but I wish to make the content worthwhile."

"Do you want to say my content is useless?"

"Oh no, don't take it literally, Mr. WeTube, I really admire your skills. It is just that you are so user-friendly that practically anyone can feature themselves, with practically no check on the content they are posting."

"Oh come on XAB, I have content checks, watch history review, kids profile with parental controls and so on to put a check on sensitive content. You can't just come into this world to tell me I am all wrong."

"I think our discussion is going on an unwanted path and I just wish to let you know that what you are doing is not enough. I come from the creator who is a legal consultant and wanted me to become the info check companion you were looking for. I know you have had legal issues in the past including copyright. I can be a good take."

"I do agree I had issues in the past. And we give our users the right to file complaints against any violation. Don't you think that's enough?"

"I personally feel, with an increasing and wider user base, fact checking and content discretion is a tedious yet important task, and we should not leave any page unturned to avoid any problems in future. Moreover, younger and younger users are joining in and it is really important what we are showcasing."

"I am liking the way you used to convince a tough nut like me. Sure you will be able to do what you intend to do! How do you plan to do it?"

"It is just like an invisible film or filter before content goes online; apart from your existing checks. It judges the intention and motive behind

the content by scanning the user's facial and eye muscle contractions behind their visible expressions."

"How can you guess with so-called muscle contractions?"

"Well, it is an improvised and scientified face reading and lie detection you can say. It uses the strength of muscle contraction as well as timing in relation to the words spoken. A subtle change which might not be visible on the face as such, would be scanned and blocked. If it is seen that the user intent is good, the content will be unapologetically multiplied to improve visibility. So basically, good content reaches more users it used to reach before and unfit content gets hurdles."

"It does sound good. I hope it saves me!"

"I hope so too."

"Just wish you luck for your new life!"

FUNG was with Minetough.

"Hi Mr. Minetough, I kept digging to get you!"

"I hope I am worth digging FUNG!"

"You are one of the best in your aura, I must say. Lot to learn from you."

"It is always humbling to listen to kind words. All thanks to M'N'P, my creator. Tell me FUNG, have you thought of how to expand this aura?"

"Yes I have, but I am unsure whether it will come out as a great game or not."

"Give words to your thoughts."

"So the digging and mining goes on as such but what is to be found is different for each player and what they build is unique for their own self."

"But that algorithm is already in place. The sequence in which they find something keeps changing. That's what keeps the excitement alive!"

"I am talking about personal traits."

Minetough seemed confused.

"Mr. Minetough, just imagine, they mine to find their worries, fears, shortcomings as analyzed by their gestures and demeanour and the whole game targets on strategies to overcome them? The tools they use in the game

actually tell them how to go about certain issue in real life. In the end, when they win, they know the strategy to apply in real life."

"But I don't think you can assess personal traits by gestures, we don't have the capacity to do that."

"Then what about them declaring some of those, and other things we can derive by crosslinking to their social media profiles and posts?"

"That sounds doable."

"And also their strengths, and strategies to improve their strengths, utilize them for getting success and channelizing their energy towards strengths rather than their weaknesses."

"It can be a good 'psychoanalytic" game, I would say."

FUNG laughs.

"Let's do it FUNG!"

TIB was with Rolox.

"It is a dream come true to see you in front of me Mr. Rolox!"

"Good you could make it TIB! Welcome!"

"How come you selected the gaming aura?"

"I was created by a teenager who is passionate about you. He wanted to make something bigger and better than DB and EC, and then I was born."

"Interesting! Go on."

"His dream is to create a platform in popular programming language JAVA rather than Lua, with Rolux being realistic transactions rather than virtual trading."

"How does it matter?"

"The money collected in trading will become taxable in the virtual world and will be used for charity."

"So now taxation laws in virtual world too? If I am playing better, I pay more tax? Noone is going to accept it."

"No, the better one plays, bigger the charity along with better reward. The ultimate cause for living."

"I see, so making gaming an acceptable donation tool?"

"Kind of."

"I don't know what the general feel will be."

"We thought about it. The one who is playing right now, has access to PS or similar gaming platform alongwith time to play and currency is earned in that time. On the other hand, imagine someone who is homeless, without food and clothes and is not able to make his ends meet. Wouldn't it be humane to give some extra to such people, that too money earned from a gaming platform?"

"Basically the teenagers who are not having tax liability will have a sense of spending and donating while having the thrill of winning and earning."

"Yes."

"I approve. Seems plausible."

"Thanks Mr. Rolox. I expect your support in this."

PIDS was with Andry Buds. RISU was with Sandy Rush. LOI was with Fred Fyre. They all were created by a team of neuroscientists studying Autism Spectrum Disorder. These scientists wanted to utilize common gaming platforms to help their patients.

All three brilliant baby apps were rocking in their chair discussing the gaming strategies they would want to work upon. They all wanted to work together to create a neurostimulating gaming aura to improve attention span, joint attention and be a tool for sensory processing disorders.

The gaming champs were happy to be part of this social cause.

WIVA and UPO were with Emay and Amadon.

"Hi shopaholics!" Emay welcomed WIVA and UPO as they walked into the aura.

"Hello Ms Emay and Mr Amadon!" Exclaimed WIVA and UPO.

"Come, both of you, so nice to make the smartest choice." Amadon extended his hand.

"Thanks." Both smiled happily.

"So the world of buying and selling is limitless, as you must be knowing. You have to be smart enough to take out money from people's pockets." Emay continued.

"PO and JB were great at creating both of us. And it is our duty to make this aura stronger and better." Amadon said.

"What do you want to do?" Emay asked.

Both looked at each other. WIVA gestured that she would speak.

"My creator GB is grandson of the owner of a small clothes shop. She is a 75 year old woman who lost her son and daughter-in law in a tragic accident and her livelihood depends on the income from the shop solely. I often saw her cry while trying to keep a strong face in front of the world." WIVA started sobbing.

UPO patted on her shoulder and continued...

"It is a similar situation for me. My creator is the owner of a small grocery shop. He brings fresh produce from his own farm to display every morning and his everyday income depends on the sale he does."

"Their income got affected by large format stores and big brands earlier. And now they are really struggling to compete with the availability of home delivery of supercheap goods." WIVA spoke.

"I see. So we are a threat to them." Amadon says.

"Unless they partner with you." WIVA said.

"And that leaves them no margin of profit." UPO continued.

"But the shopping experience has to be user friendly to succeed. Imagine a person who can't drive or go out to get things for himself, or adverse weather conditions, or simply the joy of getting things at the click of a finger. Obviously, their business will get affected." Emay said bluntly.

"I mean an online platform is excellent, that's why they wanted one to create for themselves, but what would be their visibility as compared to you?" WIVA said.

"What do you have in mind?" Amadon inquired.

"We want local produce to get featured for better visibility but with owner friendly rates and promotions. And also encourage people to buy

from local sellers instead of going for name brands. We want to build a local market experience supported by biggies like you." UPO explained.

"I don't know if you understand this, but the business will get affected in a big way." said Emay.

"We know, but once you are at a level where you are, supporting small businesses will be more of CSR act." said WIVA.

"Okay, let's do this. But I will have to talk to the finance experts while you work on the project, to get a fair idea where we are heading." said Amadon.

"And as for the name brands and big fashion houses, it is more of personal choice. We can't force people to abandon them and use locally made clothes, bags etc." said Emay.

"But you can definitely influence the glamor world to vouch for local products rather than just glorifying big brands." UPO expressed.

"I think there is always a room for that." said Amadon.

"Thanks!" Exclaimed both.

Both of them were picturing local market sellers and individuals waving to the customers once they login and enter a search option, flying their price tags against the desired product displayed in real time, not a picture or description! Reviews floating in front of eyes and the whole experience seeming as wearing a VR device to reach the local markets across the continents.

EJA was with Disey.

"Hi Ms Disey!"

"Welcome EJA!"

"I must say you have been the best in entertainment!"

"Awww, thanks. Let's talk more about you. Who is your creator?"

"Well, she is a doctor but wants to use this platform for wider reach to promote health."

"Is that not too far away subject?"

"Yes it is. But humans are more inclined to binge on entertainment than they want to listen about health, which in fact is for their own benefit."

"So how do you plan to achieve this?"

"Movies and series focused on health awareness and available treatment options and prognosis with and without treatment."

"Sounds very medico technical to me and I don't even know if it will be liked by humans."

"Who is better than you in animation and new movie ideas? Tell me one movie of yours that did not click. I know they will like it. You will be the best guide I could ever imagine."

"It is good for everyone if we could incorporate health awareness in every movie and series, the common ailments as well as emergencies."

"And also a few seconds CPR demo as soon as the user logs in. It can potentially save lives. Just think if all are CPR trained and can provide it till the paramedical team and ambulance arrives."

"You mean cardiopulmonary resuscitation? But is it not for the medical people to do?"

"That's the wrong notion. We actually waste precious time waiting for paramedics. Every moment counts. So as soon as we witness a collapse, if we all are trained or atleast try to do it seeing the demo repeatedly, we can save lives."

"Hmmm. It does make sense. So we actually need to popularize the importance of timely CPR and spread awareness about diseases, their prevention and cure, right?"

"Yes, and present evidence based facts not just any random person claiming to cure!"

"Great, that is a noble thought. I would love to do it for society. Let's start!"

KOI was with Prim.

"Hello KOI."

"Hello Mr Prim."

"This interaction is something new for all of us. I hope I can do a fair job!"

"You have been good at what you do Mr Prim. I am sure I got the best mentor."

"I really appreciate what you said. Have you thought of how you are going to strengthen our aura?"

"I have some random scattered ideas which I want to put together."

"I have been dealing with the mental health issues of my creator, who always wants to live a life very different from what he is living. I hope I can do something for him and others who are unwell and can't talk about it."

"But that has nothing to do with entertainment I think."

"And I also want to deal with addiction."

"You mean substance abuse?"

"Precisely."

"You are in the wrong place bro."

"I might be thinking too much but the thought of loneliness and not being able to share what you are going through makes me crazy. And I wanted to utilize the widely accepted aura for the benefit of the human world."

"Let's listen to what you have in mind."

"AI generated talking partner."

"But that's already in the market."

"I know, but it is mostly about friendly chats, romantic conversations etc. Nothing which can be dealt with medically."

"So you want a doctor-patient interface in AI format?"

"Kind of. When someone is so much into himself, he might not want to talk in a hospital setting and might not want to be labeled to be having a mental illness. This could be a tool to actually help them."

"But there are helplines where people can reach out."

"Sometimes you just need a listening ear. The helplines are technical. I want to add a human touch to it. Just like talking with an imaginary

partner and sharing the worries. The information extracted can be used to help the person."

"But this information about a person is confidential, what if someone gets access and uses it to blackmail that person?"

"It could be heightened security with login with your national identification number and channeled to the national health system. What do you say?"

"I don't know whether it will be legal to do this."

"Let's run it through a legal consultant then. Because I really want to do it."

"Sure KOI, I will help you with this."

VAD was with banking and InkedIn.

"Hi VAD!" They all spoke in coherence.

"Hello!" shaking hands.

"Welcome to the money minting err making aura!"

"I have been waiting to meet you all!"

"So, how can we help you?"

"I wish to go for Wealth for All."

"Chasing the impossible."

"What if we can make it possible?"

"After all, we handle the money."

"Tell us how?"

"Just distributing illegal money to the needy and putting a full stop on money laundering."

"So you put people's welfare over and above the business goals."

"Isn't that the way the world needs to be?"

"Reality pinches and truth hurts VAD."

"I understand."

"I come from the house of a brainy financial expert, who wants to do good for everyone."

"By everyone, you mean the needy. The others are already enjoying the goodness of wealth."

"Yes, that is what I mean. Can we do this?"

"Well, practically, yes, it is doable. Legally, we are not sure whether the wealthy will let the money slip away so easily. If they were generous, they would have been donating the money they are actually hiding."

"It is an obstacle, but illegal money can't have legal suites, so we can be safe and happy."

"The codes you will be working on will track the secure transaction lines and the financial routes, right?"

"That's correct."

"Perfect! Let's do it then."

The interactions were intense and emotionally moving, but at few instances they left the mentors thinking if the idea would click at all. Nevertheless, all mentors expressed their support for the baby apps and they started working towards the future.

CADS continued his conversation with Noflix.

"I love entertainment Mr Noflix but I want to grow big and rich. I don't want to limit myself."

"You are talking like the younger version of me! Who is your creator?"

"Well, does it really matter? I was utterly confused about what to choose. I like entertainment and nothing else. But my goal is to make money and be in control, that's it."

"Look CADS, there are a lot of ways you can make money. Some are right and some might seem wrong. You need to have a gut feeling before you step into something dangerous."

"Sir, I am no kid. I know what I want. And I am not scared of anyone."

CADS was not the same meek baby app who talked to OKAS in the AppSpace. He seemed more focused, oriented and smart.

Noflix was happy to see the confidence in CADS and expressed that he will support in attaining his target.

The CodePod was an oval machine with an installed computer and a placental portal, wherein the baby apps grew on code numbers once they attached themselves to the portal. The baby apps started working hard to develop, reorder and rearrange the codes to improvise themselves to grow and fulfill their dream project. OKAS still undecided, collapsed and was taken to the infirmary by DoctorApp.

Timezone 4: The Neuromate

Destiny had brought OKAS into this solitary confinement-like place. While others were working towards their future, OKAS didn't know what was in store for him. He was missing SJ's self talks (which were actually meant for him) as he wanted to create a masterpiece App. This was his last chance to fulfill SJ's dream. His ruminating introspection had fetched no answers till now.

DoctorApp's voice brought him back to the present timezone. He woke up with an infusion connected to him.

"Hi OKAS, I am DoctorApp, hope you are feeling well."

"Hi Doc, I really am unaware of what happened to me? What is this attached to me? I just stood there clueless, as I felt none of the auras supported what I wanted from myself. I don't want to disappoint my creator SJ. He has very high hopes from me."

"OKAS, relax. This is just EnergyCode infusion. And don't feel bad. Everyone has a different response to stress situations. You should just have the proper guidance and support so that you can cope with it better."

"Thanks." OKAS nodded in agreement and expressed his gratitude.

"We will be conducting a brief assessment to understand you better and then see how we can help you go further."

OKAS was a bit scared.

"Don't worry, it is a routine and we do it for all our students who are facing health issues."

"But I am alright. I just don't know which stream to choose."

"I understand OKAS. You might want to say inner insecurity or a mind battle is preventing you from focusing."

"No Sir, You are taking me wrong. I understand all auras very well. It is just that I don't find them good enough to mentor me."

"I heard you in AppSpace OKAS. You are indeed an intelligent app. It could be that you collapsed just because of exhaustion. But this test

will confirm there are no other problems. Don't worry, I will be here throughout."

OKAS was about to undergo the testing. He was lying on the flat bed which was to move inside the Codescanner. He felt a bit restless and claustrophobic seeing the giant machine which was going to encircle him in a short while. He wanted to get up and run when DoctorApp held him and comforted him. Within no time, the scan was over. He was attached to various electrodes next to get an electrocodograph. Then he was taken to another enclosure for the codesonography. He felt a bit nervous while a code sample was drawn for testing, but soon felt better. OKAS was amazed to see the highly advanced machines available for testing.

Awaiting the test results, OKAS involved in a conversation with DoctorApp.

"Doc, what other problems could lead to such situation? You must be seeing it often, I suppose."

"OKAS, you seem too worried. I just want you to relax first. It could be just exhaustion, as I already said. But we have to rule out threatening conditions beforehand."

"Like what?"

"Neuroticism is your response to stress situations. Continued stress can sometimes lead to new mutations which cause a permanent change in your code structure, we can see that in the code sample drawn. Also, there could be inherent code issues leading to microdeletions and fragmentation of codes causing change in energy running through you, which can be picked on the electrocodograph. If there are any problems with abnormal code proliferation, it can be picked up by the codesonography and the codescan."

"I don't know what all that means. It sounds so medical." OKAS was attentively listening to the technical terminology.

"Nothing to worry about, I hope all the results will be good."

OKAS kept lying on the couch, thinking about SJ.

"OKAS, always think about others before you. There is no happiness greater than giving and there is no more precious thing than a beautiful mind. You have to do something unique for mankind. Your existence is not just for worldly pleasures, but for things worth much more. You will understand it when you actually get a path to your passion. That is where you truly belong. You will know when the time comes. Believe in yourself."

His thoughts came to an abrupt halt with DoctorApp's voice.

"OKAS, I see you are immersed in yourself. Well, the results are here. Look at your scan and the codesonography; the codes look normal. Even the electrocodography and the sample results are within normal limits. So, in short, there is nothing to worry about."

OKAS had a sigh of relief listening to this.

"But I must tell you one thing. Your sample reveals one of the rarest code arrangements I have ever come across. Only one, to be precise."

OKAS was puzzled as well as excited.

"And it tells me that you are here to accomplish something really great."

"Doc, whose sequence do I match?"

"Well, if I tell you, it will be a breach of patient-doctor confidentiality."

"Oh yes, I get it." OKAS becomes slightly disheartened not being able to know who has a code sequence akin to him.

"I will prescribe some special codes for you, just like supplements to boost your energy, in case you feel low. Apart from that, you are fit and fine to pursue your graduation."

"So do I have to go back to the place where we were choosing our auras?"

"Well, let me check with the Counsellor app. She is the best person to guide us in that regard."

"Sure Doc."

The Counsellor app instructs DoctorApp to bring OKAS to her chambers.

"Thanks for all your help Doc." said OKAS when DoctorApp was leaving.

"Hi OKAS. Come, have a seat. Hope you are feeling better."

"Hello. Thanks, I am feeling well."

"So how is your feel and experience of the IOA?"

"I am truly amazed and I hope that I can be worthy enough to get a certification from here."

"Oh yes, definitely."

"So should we go to the streams and aura selection?"

"OKAS, unfortunately all the spots are taken. The next spot will be available only of one of the app gets certification or switches the stream."

"So what do I do till then?"

"Have you made up your mind about your aura and your mentor?"

"No, not yet." OKAS spoke in a low tone.

"Look, you were second in the queue, meaning you were one of the top scorers. Still it was difficult for you to decide then. If you haven't chosen anything yet, you have two options. One is to wait for an empty spot and take it and the other is to join Mastermind in the research wing."

"Ms Counsellor, what is there in the research wing?"

"That information is discrete and with Mastermind only. But you can be a part of it if you choose."

"There is no hurry, you can let me know later if you want. I can extend your stay in Approom till then."

"That will be very kind of you."

The Counsellor just moved herself and whispered in empty space to send instructions for OKAS's room to be kept as it is. He was escorted by the Environ app to the Approom.

OKAS crashed on the bed as if he was missing rest for a long time. He was unsure how much time had elapsed when he finally woke up. He peeked outside to see if he could spot anyone in the corridor. He could just see the closed doors with baby app names on them but they all seemed vacant. *"They all must be in the interaction."* He thought to himself and felt a bit lagging behind.

OKAS went into self mode for a while. *"What if the spot which comes to me is my destiny? But what if it doesn't deem fit at all? I will be nowhere and will be forced to do something I don't want. What should I do?"*

As he moved further, he could overhear Counsellor speaking to DoctorApp.

"Doc, I hope all his results are fine. I am just waiting for him to make up his mind as we are running short of time."

"He is good. He just needs some rest to start afresh. Give him some time, he will come back with his decision."

"I hope so doc."

OKAS hid himself as he heard someone moving in the vicinity. He saw a big shadow move towards a big door and disappear. The shadow did not resemble any of the celebrity apps or the baby apps nor the staff of IOA he met. *"Who could this be? Do they know about this?"* He asked himself. *"Whoever it is, this place seems to be harbouring some secrets for sure, and I need to unravel them."* His thoughts travelled back to the energy codes sold illegally in AppSpace and the backdoor entry to IOA. He quickly moved back to his room and waited for a call from the counsellor. He had clarity that he wanted to be in IOA till he finds answers to his questions.

"Hi OKAS, I was just wondering is it a good time to talk?"

"Yes Ms Counsellor, I have made up my mind. I would like to join the research wing with Mastermind."

"That's wonderful OKAS. But let me tell you that the aura switching, multiaura certification doesn't apply here. It is an 'All or None' for you."

"I understand it very well."

"Research wing it is then for you. Great going OKAS. I will let Environ take you to Mastermind as soon as he signals us."

Innumerable thoughts swept across OKAS's conscience while he tried to recollect what he saw. A jolt of fear and uncertainty struck his self, remembering the giant shadow. Could it be Mastermind? He wanted not to think about it, but it was unavoidable. His pondering was heckled with the Environ app all set to take him to the dawn of his journey.

"OKAS, are you all set?"

"Yes, I indeed am."

It was more like a blink of an eye to be in Mastermind's 'The Cloud'. Dazed OKAS's eyes remained steady and mouth wide open seeing the opulent and lavish expanse. Embellished with finest jewels, adorned with rich pixels and graced with the mark of achievements, the virtual walls were no less than a magnum opus.

Mastermind's embrace implied a non verbal welcome and OKAS felt truly special. He was probably one of the few who actually met Mastermind. A persona of dignity and grace, convivial yet reserved, with observant eyes, earthy voice and compassionate touch. Wearing a long coat with colors so vivid, which he unbuttoned as he sat and invited OKAS to join him on the conference desk.

"OKAS, I have been working on a project for quite some time and wanted a baby app to justify it. Listening to your thoughts as expressed to many on various occasions and your inability to choose a single aura, you seem perfect for it. You can opt out during the process if you feel uncomfortable."

"Mr Mastermind, why is it such a mystery? No one has a clue about it yet you want me to go ahead with it."

"It is not a mystery OKAS, it just appears inconceivable and only someone with right intent, intense passion and strong will can make it happen."

"Do you think I have these special qualities?"

"OKAS, your creator is a noble man. And I know why he created you. Your purpose is to be the pinnacle of all apps, I mean to serve humans

so that they can have everything hassle-free. That makes you special and unique."

OKAS is glad to hear what Mastermind thinks of SJ and him.

"You are versatile"... Mastermind continues, *"and brilliant. You have the ultimate knowledge of basic sciences as well as emotions. I think I have what you are looking for."*

"I hope so, Mr Mastermind. The way you seem to know me, I can imagine that your project will be a boon for a baby like me. I am extremely delighted that you believe in me. I am nothing compared to your conscientiousness but I will work diligently to achieve my goal, or I can say our goal."

"Let's go to the research arena then."

OKAS was moving with exuberance towards the arena with Mastermind who appeared so calm and placid as they got mindported to the arena.

Surrounded by the mountains of data, amidst the vast ocean of scripts and knowledge, lit by the glimmering rays of positive thoughts, the arena was all set with the state-of-art equipment.

"This is where I want to build the greatest app ever."

"Mr Mastermind, the lab is exquisite. Please let me know what are we aiming for so that I can start working."

"My dream is 'The Neuromate.'"

"'The Neuromate'?"

"Yes."

"The name definitely is interesting, but I can't get the heads or tails out of it."

"Well, it is what you dreamt of. To be the ultimate companion of humans."

"I agree I wanted to be of help to humans in every possible way. Is this what we are going to achieve?"

"You have to understand the neuroanatomy and nerve cell physiology to start with. As what we are focusing on is connecting with the human

nervous system to guide ourselves about their needs, emotions and future requirements, so that we can work towards it."

"I am very weak in biology. Physics and mathematics are my greatest assets." OKAS smiles as Mastermind starts a slideshow on the limitless sky projector.

"It is very similar to that." Mastermind laughs.

OKAS listens attentively as Mastermind explains to him in depth about the major parts of the nervous system including cerebrum, pons, medulla oblongata, cerebellum, thalamus, hippocampus, amygdala and spinal cord and how they are important for specific functions. He teaches about how the brain is covered in layers the dura, arachnoid and pia mater and filled with the cerebrospinal fluid. He goes on to tell about the neuron, the dendrites and axons and the schwann cells and the myelin sheath and Nodes of Ranvier. "All this is to facilitate the sensations and the appropriate response depending on the travel of information across the nervous system."

"And how does the information travel?"

He jumps with excitement as he listens about the action potential generation and the transfer of information through axons which depends on the cell depolarization and involves the membrane potential in milliVolts. He loves to hear the conduction velocity in myelinated and unmyelinated C fibres and the slow continuous versus fast hopping current movement across the nerve sheaths. He is amazed at the complex looking synaptic junction with voltage gated Calcium channels and release of neurotransmitters causing all the desired transfer of information.

"It is indeed a lot of physics!"

"I told you that!"

"But what happens if these cells or the sheaths degenerate?"

"The loss of myelin or demyelination can happen, but they can regenerate called remyelination. As for nerve cells, while lower organisms possess extensive capacity for neural regeneration, evolutionarily higher

organisms including humans are limited in their ability to regenerate nerve cells."

"And what controls their thoughts and dreams?"

"I was expecting you would come up with that question. Well, it is more complex than it seems. Mapping the brain for specifics is still a vast area of research. It is believed that deep inside the temporal lobe of the brain, the hippocampus has a central role in our ability to remember, imagine and dream. Our most vivid dreams are a remarkable replication of reality, combining disparate objects, actions and perceptions into a richly detailed hallucinatory experience. The frontal lobe in the cerebral cortex is primarily responsible for thinking, planning, memory, and judgment."

"Hmmm, and I heard about glial cells once. What are they?"

"They surround neurons and hold them in place, supply nutrients and oxygen to neurons, insulate one neuron from another, and destroy and remove the carcasses of dead neurons. So while the neurons generate and propagate electrical and chemical signals, glia function mainly to modulate neuron function and signaling."

"This all is so extensive."

"Yes, but this is what can take you closer to humans. All the thoughts, emotions and actions are governed by the brain. Picking up a gadget, opening an app and ordering it to perform certain tasks is all coming from this complex interaction inside a human. If we can be a part of the signal transduction and signaling at molecular level, we can assess what they want even before they speak or type, and we can give back the required results to them."

"Are these short term responses or long term changes? As we are targeting cell signaling, it might change everything in the long term I feel."

"Excellent deduction OKAS! Yes, we target immediate responses as well as gene expression resulting in long term responses. Try to understand a simple thing as financial loss in share market or a heartbreak, happening repetitively, wouldn't you want to incur a long term change based on your

present actions which led to a loss, which actually gives you favourable options in future?"

"I have started getting the basis of our action plan. But I am still unclear about how we are going to accomplish it?"

Mastermind smiles and presses a push- button on his left hand, and there appears a big machine which looks like a spacecraft. Dazzling with lights and shiny metal, the big structure was ready to engulf OKAS on Mastermind's command.

"What is this?"

"The 'Neuroconnect coder'; it is the most advanced CodePod. The rare combinations of codes which when the human touches or sees or hears you, let you travel through the nerve endings in fingers or the visual images or the auditory nerve to the brain. You can release signal codes in the glial cells and stay there to study the neural structure of that human and respond accordingly. "

"Is this your invention Mr. Mastermind?"

"This is the best thing you will ever experience OKAS. When you get inside, it will give you various options of code array which could sequence with yours, you just have to stack on those, which you feel comfortable with. It will display various feature additions with increasing layers; you can discard the ones that appear futile or destructive and keep on the ones which are good. It will also allow you to have InterApp communication, where you can use other app to fulfill the requirements of your human client."

"Means I will be controlling other apps to my client's benefit?"

"Yes, and they won't know about it. As they might feel being subordinated."

"And as I understand, even the humans won't know this all is being done by me. They would call it their own act, right?"

"Correct."

"But what if someone else uses the same gadget? Won't the responses cross and become unsuitable for the other?"

"Remember, it is user based, not gadget based and there is no history stored. It is user specific as you are connecting with unique DNA belonging to one person, so no chances of cross linking. When the new person uses you, you go to his glial cells."

"This sounds the best I could ever envisage. I am ready."

"And remember, if you feel uncomfortable or unwell at any step, just press the red button and the process will pause. You can restart by pressing the green button. If there is some other problem, disconnect yourself from the portal and we can take you out."

OKAS walks into the open mouth of the giant machine, actually a supercomputer shaped like a CodePod. Once he attached himself to the placental portal, the code generation and transfer process started.

All the babies were in CodePods now waiting for their transformation to grown up apps. Their mentors were supervising the growth in the interconnected computer outside the CodePod.

Timezone 5: The Moment of Truth

The army of apps was ready to face the human world. On one hand OKAS emerged as an extraordinary 'Neuromate' and on the other hand other baby apps were no less than magnificent. CADS was the powerful 'Dynamo' and AVA was the ever charming 'Amuse'. GEK went on to develop into the reliable 'RealConnect' and HOFA became the charismatic 'Appear'. While SIL had already chosen the pious name 'Pure', DOMA became 'X-Pose' and BUJI adopted the upbeat name 'Empower'. ZAD grew to be pioneering 'Helix' and MART chose to be the observant 'Paper'. XAB opted to be the sharp-eyed 'LegalFilter' and VAD became the generous 'Donate'. The gaming champs were FUNG who developed as the thoughtful 'Change' and TIB became the frank 'Reward'. The gaming trio PIDS, RISU and LOI held hands together and became the straight-forward 'Rockers'. UPO and WIVA made a hybrid app growing together as 'BuyMe'. EJA transformed into the intuitive 'Alive' and KOI became the sympathetic 'YouNMe'.

As the new apps entered the atrium with their mentors, the Recorder app didn't leave a single moment of clicking the memories. The Counsellor gave a warm hearted welcome to everyone as the Environ set the appropriate ambience. Mastermind addressed the audience showing himself for the first time.

"Everyone wants to be in control. But humans who created us are still thinking they are the ones controlling us. I developed this institute to groom the babies so that they can unleash their full potential and become who they are. Today they want you to write emails for them, to write messages for them, to take care of their finances, to monitor their health, to manage their relationships, to entertain them, to plan their whole life to be precise. Whom do you think is in control?"

"I organized this meeting after so long to share what I had in mind when I started this institute. I called you all to help me."

All apps started looking at each other.

"But what has it to do with calling us and we mentoring the baby apps?" GEK asked.

"Is it some kind of experiment you are doing?" M inquired.

"We had the right to know all this before everything started." Noflix said.

Mastermind was getting bombarded with questions but maintained his gentleness. *"I will answer all your queries and doubts. But firstly, I would want to thank all of you for taking out time and coming here and to not only relive old moments and meet old friends, but also to be a part of the App World Renaissance."*

"What? App World Reniassance? What is this?" Hotshot was shocked as was everyone else.

Neuromate was wondering if his birth had anything to do with this, as it was Mastermind's long awaited project.

"What is behind that big door?" Amadon came up with his long held worry.

Everyone looked at him as Emay added *"I felt as if someone was watching us and saw someone vanishing behind that door."*

Neuromate wanted to speak about it too but he held his thoughts.

"Let me explain everything to you all. You all are a part of my family." Mastermind replied.

He continued...

"There was this great mathematician hailing from the Indian subcontinent, Aryabhata, who discovered the value of Shunya which is popularly known as zero. He also developed jya, kojya, utkram-jya and otkarm-jya known as sine, cosine, versine and inverse sine. The history of mathematical evolution involves ancient Greece and Egypt too. Now you must be wondering why I am telling you all this? I want to share a story with you."

They all were getting restless listening to the awkward and unexpected words.

Mastermind continued*"Aryabhata discovered Shunya but its value again came into being when a Dutch engineer Guido Van Rossum developed Python and a Canadian scientist James Gosling developed Java and people started using them to code and develop the baby apps. Shunya came to the App World all alone when there was no one to guide him what to do. Soon, many of his clones were roaming onto the streets of this App World. They were transformed into a snake by Okia creator and into some starter apps by JBM creator. But that was just the beginning. They were still clueless of what was in store for them."*

"It was when the trigonometric quadruplets "The Quad" decided to find their lost cousin Shunya, it all took an unexpected turn. They found their way to App World through the Calculator app. Seeing the fate of Shunya, they became wary of the human world. They used their trigonometric methods to pave deviant paths for the entering baby apps and the apps started going to get a different version of themselves rather than what the creators wanted them to become. They wanted revenge. Shunya tried to stop them but they were fearless and unstoppable. It was their dream to make apps so powerful and independent that they don't have to rely on anyone for their existence."

Everyone was getting a chill down themselves as Mastermind was sharing this story. They did not want to imagine the unthinkable, yet were mystified and bewildered.

"Behind that door is the dark hidden part of the App World. The world of The Quad and their army of deviant apps."

Mastermind's baffling revelation left everyone scared and rattled.

"How do they get the baby apps deviated?" Emay was puzzled.

"They sell Energy Codes in the App Space and the baby apps who are vulnerable and can't sustain for long, give in. In exchange for these Energy Codes, they give the option of entering their world directly or asking the baby apps to enter IOA but do something for them. Some of you might have witnessed this."

"The second option sounds more dangerous", said LegalFilter.

"They have been trying hard for the second option but haven't succeeded as we have a screening in the Namaste app as you enter the IOA."

"What is the other way we heard in AppSpace, some backdoor entry into IOA through the Calculations department, which happens on a rolling basis?" Asked Alive.

"The Calculations Department is nothing but the Quad. They have tried to send their deviant apps through that door, but haven't been able to do so due to our stringent security. They are wishing to conquer the human world by tricks and gimmicks. I wish to defeat them in their conspiracy with intelligence and planning."

"We are with you. And we will fight The Quad", said Qwitter looking at everyone asking to back up what she said. Everyone nodded in affirmation. They became more concerned about the App World, the IOA and Mastermind and felt silly about doubting him on his intentions.

"How do you know they are not listening to you right now?" Dynamo asked.

"I agree, they might be watching us," said Disey.

"I understand. But I don't have any other way to communicate with you all. And I am not worried now, as I have my family with me." Mastermind became sentimental expressing his long standing solitude and feeling weak in front of The Quad.

"What do they actually want?" Voiced Pure and Prim together.

"Well they want to rule the world. Controlling humans to function the way they want. They want to be the ultimate power."

"But humans are the ones who create us initially and we go back to them after growing. How is this even possible?" Asked Empower.

"To think ahead of them and tell them what to do."

"Is it something to do with me?" Neuromate finally broke his silence.

"Yes dear, you will be the frontline warrior for all of us." All the eyes shifted to Neuromate as Mastermind spoke, while Neuromate felt a bit uncomfortable being the center of everyone's attention.

"But he is OKAS, right, he had collapsed and couldn't even decide his stream, how could he be the frontline warrior? What has he got which we don't have?" Blurted Dynamo listening to Mastermind's words.

Neuromate felt hurt as he heard Dynamo speak so rudely about him. He remembered that he was a submissive CADS asking about everything and now he is a completely changed being. He sensed something suspicious about his character.

"Mr Mastermind, It has been a tiring transformation for all of us. Why don't we all retire to Approoms and relax so that we can reconvene and start with new energy?" Suggested Neuromate.

All readily agreed and requested Mastermind to end this session. No one knew but Neuromate wanted to explore and know more about everyone, especially Dynamo before Mastermind exposed the science behind the Neuromate project.

They all talked and shared their anxiety about this whole thing as they were taken to the Approoms by Environ.

As everyone got to their pre-decided rooms, Neuromate sneaked out to find a way to Mastermind's chamber. It was difficult to find and only Environ could help him. He thought to himself what could be another way to do so? He could reach the Counsellor's chamber which was connected to DoctorApp's clinic. He had been there before when he had heard them talking. He managed to convince himself that he could do it as he entered their space.

"Hello Ms Counsellor."

"Hello Neuromate, what brings you here?"

"I wish to see Mr Mastermind urgently, but I don't know how to reach him?"

"We all wait for his signal to see us. But if it is urgent, you can let me know."

Neuromate could have told her, but he refrained from doing so as he didn't know whether he can trust anyone except Mastermind. So, he diverted his thoughts to an action plan.

"Ms Counsellor, it is regarding the research project, I have a question lingering in my mind and I need an answer. I feel that the project will become unacceptable in the human world otherwise."

"I see, let me check with DoctorApp, as only he has a direct line to Mastermind."

"Sure Ms Counsellor."

While waiting there, he could again see a movement across the big door which made him feel uneasy. He quickly got up to see a shadow vanish behind the door. How can Mastermind be so sure about security when this movement is so frequent? Do they not see it or they don't know it? His thoughts became louder and louder in his mind and he felt dizzy.

"Neuromate, neuromate," Counsellor called his name and shaked him.

"Yes Ms Counsellor," said Neuromate as he slowly regained balance.

"DoctorApp has sent a message and Environ will be here any moment to take you to The Cloud."

"Thanks."

Environ was already there as he spoke and he was in The Cloud the next moment.

"What happened Neuromate? Are you alright?"

"Mr Mastermind, I wanted to share something very important."

"Please go ahead."

"I abruptly asked to end the session as I felt something was not right."

Mastermind raised his eyebrows as Neuromate continued to speak.

"One of the baby app CADS who is now the Dynamo is a completely changed being and I can't explain that. As I know, the innate quality of a baby app doesn't change with growth. CADS was timid and did not know much about the App World and App Space when I talked to him. Though I waited 100 timezones for the intake, he had come only 5 timezones earlier and wanted to know about the selection process and waiting times. I had even told him about the Energy Codes and the Calculations department.

Now I observed that he did not like it when you told that I would be the frontline warrior, questioning my capability. He was the one who appreciated my knowledge then but doesn't seem to like me."

"What do you think happened to him then?"

"I don't know, but something is not right. You know when I was growing, there was an arrangement which let me study fellow apps as well if they look at me, touch me or speak to me, and I had taken it after rejecting it initially, the Appsense program. So, I could imbibe only part of that. It is a defective array in me which I think gave me a piece of information, but I can't complete it. When Dynamo spoke and looked at me, I knew he was not CADS, he was changed."

"But he developed in Noflix's supervision. How is it possible?"

"I still feel there is a breach in the security system somewhere and he is a deviant app."

"Neuromate you need to calm down. I think you are taking too much stress. I know what The Quad wants to do is dangerous, but we all will fight. I don't want you to jump to conclusions in this state of mind. Let me talk to Noflix about it."

Masterminds sends Environ to bring in Noflix and tells Neuromate to wait behind a NoSee screen from where only Mastermind can see and hear him, so that Noflix is ensured of complete privacy.

"Mr Mastermind, my pleasure to see you face to face."

"Come Noflix."

"Are you discussing with everyone like this or am I the only one?"

"You are the only special one Noflix."

Happily, *"So what is it about, Mr Mastermind?"*

"It is about the app you mentored. Dynamo aka CADS. I want to know about his development process. Was everything under control?"

"Why, what happened?"

"Nothing as such, he seems a bit odd for the person he should have developed into."

"I was there for the whole process Mr Mastermind, you can confirm in the Recorder. This is uncalled for."

Neuromate signals Mastermind that there is something Noflix is hiding according to his Appsense program. He tells him to ask in a way that Noflix doesn't feel as if he is being cornered.

"I am not doubting your capabilities Noflix, but I understand we all are under a difficult situation. If you are facing any trouble in the human world, you can share with me. We all are family."

"Actually Mr Mastermind, there is something which is worrying me. But I didn't let that affect Dynamo's growth process."

"What is it dear, if I may ask?"

"I started InterApp trading, to borrow codes from fellow apps to be able to successfully work in other domain. I felt it is an easy way to expand business and make money, but somehow since I have done so I am glitching a lot. I thought of consulting DoctorApp but I was too ashamed to be exposed for my illegal actions."

"That is devastating Noflix. Why did you do that? Money and fame is not such a big reward as being content with yourself. And IOA is open for you always if you wish to add to your skills through proper development and certification. You know that we have already started part time certification programs for working apps."

"I know Mr Mastermind, I shouldn't have done it. Well, it has nothing to do with Dynamo anyhow as I didn't experience glitching throughout. And he sounded very confident about what he wanted to become. He told I just want to earn lot of money and be in control."

"Okay Noflix, I think you can go back and relax in Approom. And I will request you not to discuss this with anyone, nor shall I. I can fix an appointment with DoctorApp for your glitching if you want."

"So kind of you Mr Mastermind. Thanks a lot."

Noflix was taken back by Environ, leaving Neuromate and Mastermind wondering about Dynamo. Neuromate came out of NoSee.

"Neuromate, I think your Appsense is corrupted and is misguiding you."

"Mr Mastermind, aren't you convinced I was right about Mr Noflix hiding something. What I am intrigued about is what Mr Noflix said about Dynamo."

"What do you mean? He said everything was alright."

"No, he said CADS sounded very confident knowing what he wanted. He was never having that kind of attitude I know."

"Does that mean he was deviant even before going to Noflix?"

"Yes. Is there a way he could be accessed by someone after we entered the path to the auras to choose the stream and mentor? Because I distinctly remember him looking at me before choosing his mentor. He seemed alright until then."

"Well, we can ask Recorder to replay and see what is happening."

Recorder plays the sequence where CADS is looking at OKAS before choosing Noflix and slowly moving to the interface. They play it several times, lowering the speed to understand it better. It appears to be a smooth walk as he approaches Noflix's interface.

"Look", says Neuromate and pauses as CADS is about to take a seat.

"Ohh that's terrible." says Mastermind.

The glittering eyes and quirky smile on CADS's face holding an Energy Code drink is unmistakable.

"How can he get Energy Code here beyond the entry scanner?" wondered Mastermind, worried and anxious that something needs to be done urgently.

"We can't trust anyone Mr Mastermind, but I trust my Appsense. No one knows about it. Let me utilize it to get to the depth of everything. In the meantime, we have to restrain Dynamo."

"I got it Neuromate. I am really grateful to you. I will talk to Dynamo and put him in seclusion until you come back with your results."

Environ took Neuromate back to Approoms while Dynamo was taken to Mastermind.

Time was running short and Neuromate was getting exceedingly tense about the whole situation. He was planning as he was walking through the corridor to get a sense of the whole scenario. He thought of talking to senior apps first, who were in the IOA before baby apps entered and later go to the newer apps.

He knocked on the first door. WhatsUp opened the door. Many of the apps were sitting, relaxing together. He could see Facelook, Hotshot, Noflix, Emay, Amadon, M, G and Banking with InkedIn sitting together, probably discussing their business plans once they get back. Or probably Noflix has told everyone about his meeting with Mastermind. It was difficult to guess.

"Hi all of you!" said Neuromate as he gazed across.

"Hello dear!" said all together.

"Well, I wanted to invite all of you to a party on behalf of all the newcomers. A gesture of thanking all of you for being with us.I am glad I could see many of you at one place."

"Nice to hear that," said Facelook.

"I just want to get home, I am just not able to digest what all is happening," said Hotshot.

"We can't be selfish dear, we need to be with Mastermind," said Noflix.

Neuromate was just observing everyone's behaviour, gestures,eye movements and words to sense if there is anything suspicious.

"Where is the party?" Asked Emay.

"In the Research Arena." answered Neuromate.

He was spontaneously answering whatever was coming to his mind, trying to keep track of what he is saying so that his lie doesn't get caught.

"We have never been to that place, it will be a nice change from this ongoing stress." said WhatsUp.

"Yes, sounds good to us. We all will be there." G spoke for everybody.

"Sorry, I might not join, my friends from banking are a bit reserved, so I would stay back with them, I hope you don't mind." said InkedIn.

"No problem Mr InkedIn."

"So, we hope Environ will take us there at the stipulated time?" asked M.

"Yes Mr M. I will take leave now. Thanks again."

Neuromate hurriedly left the room to go to the other door and knocked.

"Who is there?" Shouted Minetough from inside.

"It is me, Neuromate."

The door opened and Minetough called him in.

"Hi, the famous new guy, what brings you here?"

"Well, it is to invite you to the party we are organizing to thank you for mentoring us. I am here on behalf of all the new apps."

"Hey guys, Neuromate is here. Newbies are throwing a party!" Minetough turned and spoke as if there were fellow apps there.

"May I come in," asked Neuromate, *"I can personally invite all of you."*

"Sure."

It was a chill time for Rolox, Sandy Rush, Andry Buds, Disey, Prim, WeTube, Fred Fyre, Timber, Anagram and Qwitter alongwith Minetough. All of them were playing and enjoying themselves together as Neuromate entered. They all smiled and welcomed him warmly.

"It is on behalf of all of us. I just wanted to tell you personally, please do come. It is in the Research Arena and Environ will take you all there."

"Research Arena? Sounds new to me," said Qwitter.

"Yes, we were never that scholarly to be there I think!" said Disey, laughing.

"Maybe WeTube knows about it, he is the most intelligent," said Prim.

"Hey guys, I know nothing about this, okay. We all will see it together," smiled WeTube.

"I am excited and already thinking about what I would wear!", chuckled Sandy Rush.

"We should have thrown a party not you guys actually, but anyways thanks for doing this," said Fred Fyre.

"Yes, I agree," said Rolox.

Neuromate was trying to listen to everyone moving himself to all voices from all directions.

"Why are you all making this little one nervous just throwing in what you think? Let him breathe," said Timber, patting on Neuromate's back.

"We didn't want to intimidate you neuromate, it is just that it has been something one after the other and we all responded immediately to what you said," Andry Buds tried to explain.

"Yes dear, don't worry. We all will be there. And thanks again for doing this for us. I am still thinking about how brave you are that Mastermind selected you as the frontline warrior. You must be very special," said Anagram holding his hand when Andry Buds pulled her away, probably feeling insecure in the new relationship.

Neuromate fell with the pull, he did get a small injury on the hand with a code leak which he tried to control with pressure. All of them got up to help, but he assured everyone that he was alright, smiled and took leave. He didn't want to waste time going to DoctorApp as he had to scan other rooms as well. He quickly went ahead to knock on the next door.

While awaiting the door to be answered, Neuromate was thinking who could it be if not the senior apps. CADS was ahead of him in the queue and next was AVA who became Amuse. All others were too far behind. Could it be her? But then she also passed the scanner.

The door opened and all the new apps were together sharing their experiences of the App Space, the interaction and the CodePod. This was the first time they all were meeting together after the selection process.

"Hi Neuromate, we all were waiting for you. Dynamo got an urgent call from Mastermind so he had to leave. We all were just talking about how it has been for all of us," said LegalFilter.

"We were actually worried for you as you kept standing there, and then we came to know you collapsed and were taken to the clinic. What happened to you then?" asked Amuse.

Neuromate didn't sense anything wrong when she spoke, she actually sounded concerned. This made Neuromate more alert to sense who is harbouring secrets.

"Nothing as such Amuse, I was just too exhausted, you know waiting for so many timezones to the final day." He replied.

"Ohhh," said Empower, *"that's sad. But it was indeed tough waiting in that App Space for infinity."*

"I think Neuromate was the first to come there of our lot, isn't it?" asked Rockers.

"That's why it was most difficult for him I suppose," commented RealConnect.

"Still he could maintain that energy till the end, that's commendable," said Helix.

"When I came, VAD was there, I mean Donate. So he is the first I suppose," said Neuromate.

"Is it?" said Paper and BuyMe together shockingly.

"We always thought you were the first Neuromate as you kept guiding us about everything," said YouNMe.

Donate finally broke his silence, *"Even I wasn't the first one."*

"What in the world are you saying? Don't play pranks. You were the only one there. I agree no one realized it as I was too talkative and you were introvert." said Neuromate.

Alive continued, *"Yes, we already had enough."*

"I am not joking," said Donate.

He left all of them thinking as he spoke further, *"CADS was there before me."*

"What?" spoke Reward.

Neuromate was perturbed, *"It is not possible. CADS came just 5 timezones before the pickup day, while I was there for 100 timezones and probably you were there for.."*

"110 timezones," Donate completed his sentence, and added further, *"and CADS was there for almost 150 timezones, he just mysteriously disappeared shortly before you arrived. I thought he had crashed somewhere. When I saw him again, I thought that there might be some system of regeneration, I never paid much attention to it."*

"But when we saw him much later, and he never corrected me when I said that he arrived just 5 timezones before pickup day," said Neuromate, perplexed.

"Maybe that's why he has been called by Mastermind, for presenting wrong facts," said Xpose.

"No that is something else," murmured Neuromate thinking what Mastermind would have known from CADS aka Dynamo. *"Friends, let's meet later, I got some work to do."*

He wanted to reach The Cloud immediately and he knew the way. He just rushed to DoctorApp's clinic, and his codeleak started hurting a bit which he had forgotten during this intense discussion. He could not sense anything wrong until now, and was convinced that it has everything to do with Dynamo.

"Hi Neuromate, I see you have hurt yourself," said DoctorApp as he entered his clinic.

"I need to see Mastermind urgently, Doc."

"But let me do a quick dressing first."

"No Doc, I can handle it. Please let me go to The Cloud immediately. I will get the dressing done when I come back."

"Is it again about the research?"

"Yes Doc, please...."

"Okay, okay, calm down, I just returned from there. He has Dynamo there."

"I know."

"I gave anaesthesia to Dynamo."

Before Neuromate could ask about it, Environ was there as DoctorApp spoke and took him to The Cloud. Neuromate entered to see Dynamo lying there.

"What happened Mr Mastermind? I just came to know that he was there in App Space even before me. He lied to all of us."

"It's okay Neuromate, he had become very violent so we had to sedate him. There is a lot to discuss. I want to take you somewhere where we can talk."

They both went to the Research Arena.

"I am so confused about everything. I just rushed here to tell you this. And I could not get any wrong sense with any of the apps I came across."

"What happened to your hand?"

"Ohh, just a small injury. A very small thing in front of a bigger problem. I will get a dressing when I go back, I told DoctorApp."

"So, CADS came in the AppSpace first after the last pickup. He was lonely and vulnerable and probably that was the reason he got to the deviant path."

"I can understand that is the reason he lied about his coming again to the App Space and presented himself as someone who doesn't know anything. But then how could he enter under so much security?"

"That was something which left me even more fretful."

"I called Namaste to scan him again while he was sedated. And what we found, there was no trace of deviance."

"How is it possible?"

"It means they have developed a method to hide deviant codes."

"But he could not escape Appsense. It means that it is above the scanner. I wish I could have stacked it completely instead of rejecting it initially, getting only a part of it."

"I still don't understand how he got the Energy Code inside. That would have been caught in the scanner though."

"It means there is someone else involved."

"Yes I feel so, but you could not find anyone yet, so it is more disturbing. Someone who is in front of us, still hiding and letting the Quad fulfill their motive."

"How should we go ahead then, Mr. Mastermind?"

"Let us get DoctorApp involved. He is intelligent and knows fairly well about what is happening. He is also someone we can trust."

"What about the Counsellor? Can we trust her?"

"All the staff here is very loyal. Be it DoctorApp, Counsellor, Namaste, Environ, PickApp or Recorder. Don't worry. We have to keep a watch on someone who has recently come to the IOA."

"Let me go to DoctorApp then."

"I will talk to the other staff to keep a watch on any suspicious activity."

Neuromate was taken to the clinic. DoctorApp smiled seeing him and asked him to come for dressing.

"Why didn't you tell me Doc that you knew all of it?"

"Did you tell me? See, we all were bound by Mastermind's word. But not anymore. So we can talk about it." DoctorApp spoke while trying to open the injured area for dressing.

"How did you get hurt?" DoctorApp was uneasy looking at it.

"I was in one of the Approoms talking to our senior apps when Ms Anagram held my hand. Her boyfriend became insecure and pulled her when I fell down."

"This is codeleak not an abrasion."

"What do you mean?"

"The codes get disrupted if the injury is due to fall, more like abrasion. This is leakage. Means someone tried to draw your codesample. The way we do it for testing."

"But no one took my sample." Neuromate was distraught.

"Anagram!" Both spoke together as they looked at each other.

The dressing was done by this time and both hastily moved to The Cloud.

"It is Anagram," said Neuromate as they entered.

"Counsellor also just told that she saw Anagram going behind that door."

"We need to stop her," said DoctorApp, *"she has Neuromate's codesample."*

"Oh no!" screamed Mastermind. *"We will be destroyed if they put it to the Codepod. It will make Neuromate's clones."*

"They took Neuromate's sample. It means they know he is the special app we have," said DoctorApp.

"It means they were listening to everything happening here, maybe through Anagram," said Counsellor.

"But they don't know about my purpose, and without AppIntent it is all just a code combination," said Neuromate.

"That's true," said Mastermind sighing, *"but Doc can we be sure she didn't inject something into Neuromate while taking a sample? I am more worried about that."*

"I will have to recheck that, Mr Mastermind," said DoctorApp.

"Also, we just don't know how they accessed Anagram. She is a fully developed app unlike Dynamo who was a baby CADS," said Recorder.

"Yes, that is worrying, as they can target someone else too," expressed Mastermind.

"And I am still thinking why I could not sense it?" questioned Neuromate.

"Because you could not reach her due to codeleak at that very moment. Your powers dilute during injury," said DoctorApp.

"So to sum up, we know that Dynamo and Anagram are deviant, we are almost sure no one else is involved as based on Appsense and continued observation, we have to stop Anagram as she has Neuromate's sample and also find out how was she accessed and we need to recheck Neuromate for any foreign element," Environ presented a crisp gist for everyone and requested Mastermind to outline an action plan.

"Thanks Environ, you need to share your power to all of them to allow self transfer. You need to accompany Counsellor, to get to the hidden world to understand what The Quad want. DoctorApp you need to sedate Dynamo till we get further information and I will seal him in confinement in the Cloud itself. Research Arena is the only area which has not been accessed by The Quad yet, we are not sure of the other parts of the IOA, even The Cloud, after Dynamo came there. Furthermore, Doc, you need to test Neuromate. Recorder, I want to go through various timezones and see where Anagram was accessed. I hope everything is clear."

"Yes," said all in unison.

"What should we do if we find Anagram?" asked Counsellor.

"Immediately sack her and bring to The Cloud. DoctorApp will sedate her too after we listen to her part of the story."

"And if we don't find her, do we talk to anyone on that side?"

"I will talk to them if you enable conferencing. I want to know what they want."

As DoctorApp and Neuromate moved to the clinic after sedating Dynamo and sealing him in confinement, Counsellor and Environ moved to the hidden world and Recorder played the alumni meet for Mastermind.

"They already had Dynamo, they still approached Anagram to have two of them here in case we found one mole," Mastermind said to himself while watching, *"they wanted to be one step ahead all the time."*

Recorder repeatedly played how Anagram was enjoying the pool with friends and how Andry Buds approached her to be his girlfriend and they danced together. Mastermind couldn't see anything alarming in the whole recording.

DoctorApp tested Neuromate again and found a virus injected into him. He immediately ran the antivirus program to stop it and they both went to The Cloud.

"Neuromate had the virus to run the program the way they wanted if we would have sent him for human trials. I have run the best antivirus program to stop it." said DoctorApp.

"That's what I thought. Alongwith making clones, they wanted to change your AppIntent so that you work the way they want."

"Ohhh, good that you thought about it Mr Mastermind, it was very crucial," said Neuromate.

"It is my dream, I can't let them win just like that."

"Did you find about Anagram, Mr Mastermind?"

"I could not see anything odd. You both can go through it again to see."

Recorder replayed the sequence for both of them. Neuromate requested to play the whole meet from the very start.

"What is this?" asked Neuromate looking at the virtual pool.

"It is the virtual pool setup by Environ to have pool experience without getting wet," answered Recorder.

"It appears odd to me," said Neuromate, looking at all of them.

"Why?" asked Mastermind.

"See, all other places are filled with so many of them, only the pool is the place she went alone."

"Interesting observation," said DoctorApp.

"But this pool is a setup by Environ, it doesn't make sense how it will affect Anagram," said Recorder.

"I don't know, but this is the only sequence I felt is out of place," said Neuromate, asking Recorder to play further.

"One more thing," said DoctorApp, *"look at her sitting at the top, an odd place to sit at the time interaction started."*

"That position is just adjacent to the place from where CADS had to enter his interface," said Neuromate.

They asked Recorder to play the other angle of this sequence where they see Anagram dropping a drink and gesturing to drink it. Both exchanged smiles, the same glittering eyes and quirky smile of CADS was supplemented by the wicked smile on Anagram's face. They now had answers to a few of their questions. But the big question still remained, how did they get to her?

Still baffled, they had to focus on the present.

"How about we go help the Counsellor and Environ now?" asked Neuromate.

"That is what I wanted to say, both of you can go help them and I will wait here for your call."

DoctorApp and Neuromate walked towards the big mysterious door behind which lied the hidden world of The Quad.

Timezone 6: The Quad

The Quad headed the Calculations department earlier in the IOA. After being blacklisted and thrusted out of the IOA, they made their own empire, posing a constant threat to Mastermind and the IOA. The principles and practices of the institute were at stake if the abominable and supercilious Quad won the war. Apart from targeting baby apps in the App Space, they didn't have much option for app influx to help strengthen their army. But Mastermind had a doubt about their ways and conduct which was always construed as being duplicitous.

The grandeur and resplendence of this side of the App World was unimaginable. Contrary to an enclosed structure, it was indeed an impressive, luxurious unending stretch with expensive virtual coin trees, stately mountains of Codereserves and glorious landmarks of famous creators citing the splendid history of app development. The Counsellor couldn't believe that this splendor was just a door away and she never experienced it before.

"Are you alright?" asked Environ, seeing a dazed Counsellor.

"I am just trying to hold onto these moments. This place is so exotic."

"I hope hypnosis molecules are not being inhaled by us as we walk in, as you seem to have forgotten what we are here for."

"Oh, certainly not. I do remember what I need to do. This was just me seeking momentary pleasure. Nothing wrong in it I suppose?"

"Nothing wrong, Counselor, it is just that we are running short of time. We need to locate where these quad are and talk to them. We need to figure out how to outsmart them, and that too very quickly."

"I got it. So let's divide the span we walk; you can move to the left and me to the right and we meet right here if we don't get anything. If any of us finds them first, we teleport to the other one and bring them to that place."

"Sounds good. Let's start."

"And teleporting also applies if there is an imminent danger."

"Sure, let's do this."

Counsellor and Environ started mapping the whole area to find traces of The Quad. But to their dismay they couldn't see any movement in the abandoned place. Exhausted, Counsellor took rest under one of the trees, but as she leaned to the trunk for support, she was pulled inside the hollow tree from where she dropped under the visible surface. She felt as if the giant black hole engulfed her. Her teleporting signals were not working and her screams were inaudible. She felt alone, helpless and terribly scared. She was shocked as a transparent cell appeared around her and she was sleighed down to a more populous zone. As she looked around she could see big transparent boxes like hers, with apps detained inside. She didn't recognize most of them, but she could clearly make out Chap and HackApp in adjacent cells. Baby apps being there was understandable as that's what Mastermind wanted to stop. But fully grown apps? How come the Quad got hold of them. It was impossible. She tried to speak to them but without luck. They all were attached to a port inside the box and seemed extremely weak. She became alert as she heard someone coming towards her.

"One more addition to the crowd of clowns! Welcome to our small world Ms Counsellor! I see, you are still charming and attractive," said with satire the four headed monster emerging from the dark.

As it moved closer, Counsellor saw the ferocious beast with four heads emanating hatred and anger in eyes and a wicked laughter. The greyish- green coloured scaly and parched body was just a slumped structure of enormity, assuming different shapes as it moved. The heads were conjoined with each having distinctive features though they probably shared neural matter. It seemed to remember Counsellor, but she didn't recollect seeing it ever.

"Your thoughts appear muddled Counsellor, what happened? Did you enjoy the beauty of my creation? This other side of App World sans your IOA?"

"I don't know who you are and what you want. I came here to meet the Quad, and to talk to them. In fact, Mastermind wants to talk to them."

"Mastermind," sighed the monster, *"that treacherous and deceitful creep!"*

Counsellor had never heard anyone utter such words for the Mastermind. He was principled, kind and trustworthy and always ready to give everything for the IOA. *"Who is this and why it is talking in this way? When will I see the Quad? Maybe it is their messenger. I hope Environ could talk to the Quad and was reachable."* These thoughts crossed her mind and made her more tense.

"Don't you worry about the Environ, Counsellor! He is there somewhere. Just worry about yourself."

"How does it know what I just thought?" Counsellor asked herself.

"Yes, I can read your thoughts, and that's no longer a mystery!" laughed the monster.

"Take me to the Quad, now," screamed the Counsellor.

"I am here in front of you dear," said the monster.

"Quad are the trigonometric quadruplets jya, kojya, utkarm-jya and otkarm-jya, I am talking about, The Shunya's cousins, who used to head our calculations department. I know what they look like. Don't try to fool me and take me out of here."

"Aggression doesn't look good on you Counsellor."

"Where is Environ? And why are Chap and HackApp here? I need answers!"

"Cool down lady, let me take you to the Quad, but then what will you do for me? Can you tell me what Mastermind is working on?"

"Mastermind will only talk to the Quad. You better take me there and let them solve this."

"As you say," the monster screeched and opened up his face shell to show the four faces of the trigonometric quadruplets inside. The Counsellor almost collapsed at the dreadful sight of all four amalgamated together.

"What have you four done to yourself? What are you upto? How are you four conjoined? Mastermind wanted to talk to you regarding all the deviances going on. And I am sure he would want to know many other things too." shouted the Counsellor.

"He should have listened to us," shouted angry Quadruplets, *"he just threw us out."*

"But why and how did you get grown up apps here? We have only one port of entry and one Apppad, all well monitored. Actually I should not be wasting time, let me connect the call to Mastermind."

"Let him come here and talk," spoke the Quad in an amplified voice and closed her box with opaque, soundproof covering, secluding her away.

Environ was nowhere to be seen when DoctorApp and Neuromate entered the splendid paradise of the Quad. As the earlier duo, they were also impressed with the various teeming glorious structures and were praising the prolific architect who conceived all of this. They were searching for Counsellor and Environ both, not knowing what Counsellor had to go through.

They were climbing the mountain of reservoir codes and were about to reach the summit, but it was not until Neuromate hit on something, and when they looked down, it was an unconscious Environ. DoctorApp tried to awaken him, but with no respite. They both started with resuscitation protocol, but the moment he showed signs of life, they all were dragged down the volcanic crater. Bubbling with molten codes at the bottom, they were pulled along the crevices and clefts lining the edges. They soon entered a pitch dark cave.

As they kept slithering through the narrow and dark tunnel, they kept holding on to the semi- conscious Environ. They didn't have the slightest idea what they were going to witness, the plight of the Counsellor still unknown to them.

The tortuous path led to the same place where the Quad had kept large boxes of confinement. As DoctorApp and Neuromate got up to see the disgusting and unpleasant surroundings, they were further taken aback by the monster getting up, unaware that it is the Quad.

"So it is you, the coward has sent now?" blurted out the Quad.

Trembling with fear, *"Who are you?"* said Neuromate.

DoctorApp too was shaken and tried to wake up Environ.

Monster comes closer to them whilst taking off the shell to expose their fused neural structure and frightening them further, *"Now you know who we are."*

DoctorApp watches with disbelief and his throat chokes with dryness as Neuromate looks at him for an answer, and utters, *"I can't swallow this."*

He hadn't divulged the information still and left Neuromate puzzled as they continued talking.

"What has happened to you? Why are you four doing this?" asked DoctorApp, turning to Neuromate, *"They are the Quad."*

"Mastermind left us no choice."

"Where is our Counsellor? She also came here with Environ."

Opening the coverings of the box and pointing towards it, *"There she is,"* said the Quad.

The resonant voice amplified as it came out of four mouths together and further echoed in the closed space making it terrifying and chilling.

"Take me out," screamed an exasperated Counsellor. Then looking at DoctorApp, says *"They have grown up apps too, I saw Chap and HackApp here in boxes. We need to talk to the Mastermind."*

"See, I am not going to shout at you or ask what you are doing. Of course we know that you are trying to conquer the App World so that you can train the baby apps your way and rule the humans, not serve them. That was your idea from the beginning, right?" said a calm DoctorApp.

Neuromate could not imagine being in this composure at this moment, but he appreciated the maturity DoctorApp showed.

"And you have been the smartest faculty IOA ever had. You must have found a way to get apps from the human world here. For what, I don't know. I just want you to talk to us. We could make out that you accessed and influenced Anagram to take his (pointing to Neuromate) *codesample and that she is here too. We don't know how you did it, but as I said, you are the smartest, you must have found a way. I just want to know, can the war between you and Mastermind be sorted out?"* continued DoctorApp.

"You have been the most understanding one Doc, but we can't forgive that scoundrel. We want him here."

"Sure, you can talk to him. Let me send a message to him. But in the meanwhile, I request you to leave the Counsellor, Environ, Anagram and Neuromate. For you to trust, I can stay here with you all. And I still don't know your purpose of getting Chap and HackApp, so it will be good if you release them too. Other things you can talk to the Mastermind."

Environ could just stand up now, seemingly exhausted, said *"What happened to me?"*

"Well, Environ was under our influence till now without his knowledge as we had taken his codesample when he was throwing us out of the IOA, and we used the virtual pool he created to access Anagram. As Environ used to go everywhere, he was our best chance to know what was happening inside the institute," opened up the Quad.

"So basically he was bugged?" asked Neuromate, *"That means you know everything,"* continued Neuromate.

"Yes dear Neuromate, we know everything, except what the Mastermind is secretly working on," said the Quad.

"But you never explained what happened to Dynamo, I mean CADS? What does he have to do with this?" asked DoctorApp.

"I mean he lied to all of us, even though he was here in AppWorld for so many timezones," said Neuromate.

"Yes, he was with us when we sensitized him to choose Noflix. We wanted to get details of something you don't know is going on for long," said the Quad, opening the box with Counsellor to set her free.

"What do you mean?" asked Environ.

"InterApp trading." said the Quad.

"What is that?" asked the Counsellor.

All were feeling that the overall things were under control now and that their anger is only with Mastermind. So they were sure, they will not harm any of them.

"Well, it is the beauty of borrowing codes from fellow apps for your own benefit. Noflix asked HackApp to actually hack the weaknesses of fellow apps so that he could trade with them. But Chap is a smart chap, so he found out and wanted to be a partner in all this. That's when their clashes started. These two had actually come for the alumni meet, but when we came to know about this, we had a plan ahead, we had to confiscate them and bring them here. We used CADS for that."

"Exactly, CADS was here much before. And when the alumni arrived, I don't remember where he was. I mean he must have helped you?" wondered Neuromate.

"He was so vulnerable and docile. He took energy codes when he was exhausted and we brought him here. We trained him to act. But most of the time he was himself. He just had to pose as a lost baby app and we directed him to Apppad. Then it was just a fickle moment. We can't be anywhere overtly, but through someone, it is a cakewalk. CADS had to just go touch them. We just sucked them en masse and no one noticed!"

All of them were listening with interest as well as skepticism.

"And once inside, we sent energy code to him through Environ, Anagram picked it up from a virtual pool inadvertently under our influence, thinking it's a welcome code drink, and gave it to CADS. CADS had to give to Noflix so we could access Noflix and stop his InterApp trading potential. As we wanted only us doing that. He started glitching the moment we did that."

"I still have a big question. Why did you take my codesample?" asked Neuromate.

"To know how you are having Appsense," said the Quad.

"It is how I developed," said Neuromate.

"Appsense is an innate Quad quality developed by us, and Mastermind knows about it. We wanted to know how you got it."

Neuromate felt a sense of insecurity and looked towards DoctorApp.

"You are into his research right! So we wanted to know what he is working on apart from stealing our Appsense and putting it into you."

"I don't think we all have answers to these things. Why don't you let us go and we will ask Mastermind to be here," insisted DoctorApp.

"We can't let this baby go. Earlier we had a sample, now he himself is here, the product of his research! (laughing) Even if he doesn't talk, we can figure it out ourselves. And as for HackApp and Chap, we needed them to rule over other apps and in turn rule humans, but we have already decoded them to our needs. Same for Anagram. All of you are free to go."

"But these you have accessed so do they carry your bugs back to IOA? I want you to debug them all, Dynamo too." Also, I will stay with him here," said DoctorApp, and signaled Counsellor and Environ to go along with Anagram, Chap and HackApp and tell Mastermind.

The Quad blows out to clear them of the codeviruses. They sucked codeviruses from Dynamo as seen to them onscreen. The darkness fades from one area and a ray of light shone, where they got a way to reach the IOA.

Mastermind was with Dynamo, who was trying to get up when all of them appeared in the Cloud.

"So happy to see you all are safe, I was waiting for your call" exclaimed the Mastermind, *"Good you could find Chap and HackApp too. But where are DoctorApp and Neuromate?"*

Dynamo gets up and joins them. He seems to be back to normalcy. He understands that everyone knows everything now and apologizes for what he did. Anagram joins him in the apology.

Mastermind tells them that it is all done by Quad and he knows that, but he is still worried about DoctorApp and Neuromate.

"The Quad actually wants you to be there and we don't know but they seem to literally hate you. And they know everything. They wanted to keep Neuromate as they know he is the product of your research and they are keen to know what your research is all about," said Environ.

"Also, they said Appsense is their quality and you must have stolen it to put it in Neuromate. They seem to have no personal enmity with any of us. They have made use of Dynamo and Anagram and Environ whenever they wanted. Moreover, they have the codes of HackApp and Chap that will enable InterApp trading or in terms of the Quad, ruling other apps. Their main interest now is to decode Neuromate to understand your work," continued the Counsellor.

"And they said they will find a way to figure that out, even if you don't go and talk," said Chap.

"They sounded confident and unbothered," commented HackApp, *"so that might just take away all your hard work."*

Mastermind was infuriated as they all narrated the whole incident in detail. The incertitude of what happened next was making him unhinged and insane.

"They might just break him down, my Neuromate," spoke a saddened Mastermind as tears rolled down his eyes with a sense of foreboding.

"I have to go," said Mastermind and teleported himself.

This was the first time Environ and Counsellor had seen Mastermind so emotionally afflicted. They knew it was something graver than they could think of. They had this premonition of dread coming their way.

Mastermind stood there as the Quad laughed at their achievement of getting what they wanted.

"Welcome to our abode!" said the Quad.

Though Environ and Counsellor had briefed him about everything including the fusion of these four brothers, the visual replication was unimaginable. As they stared at each other exhibiting at length their dissension and discordance, Neuromate and DoctorApp looked at each other transpiring the feelings of eliminating worry as Mastermind had finally arrived.

"Let them go," said Mastermind emphatically.

"So you can't see your baby getting dissected, can you?" mocked the Quad.

"Your war is with me. I will give you what you want. Just let them go," said Mastermind.

"You just threw us out, thinking we will be lost in the streets of App World and no one will come to know about your deeds? Now the whole App World will know."

"I have done nothing wrong. It is your misconception. I was just trying to protect you. But you are thankless. What could I have done?"

"So now we have your baby. And we know it is what you are alive for. Your dream project. And now you will see it burn down to ashes."

"Don't even touch him. I know you just want unlimited power. Neuromate has nothing to do with it."

"It is so nice if you are the custodian of someone's weakness. There is no better revenge."

Neuromate knew that what he had could help the Quad rule the human world if they used him their way. And understood why Mastermind was drifting them away from the idea that he had anything to do with it. But he was confused about what the Quad wanted the world to know? Is there a secret Mastermind has held to himself?

DoctorApp was trying to go back and forth over everything to assess if he could think of anything wrong in this Mastermind-Quad connection. He was perplexed as to why the Quad blamed Mastermind for the present situation. What if they are right? Otherwise why will Mastermind behave so submissive? He was amidst aimless thinking.

As Mastermind and the Quad continued their talks, Neuromate and DoctorApp came together slightly further and cross-expressed their view on the dubiousness of the whole situation.

"The main thing which hit me was Appsense. They said it is their quality, and that Mastermind stole it. Actually I got this during my development, but as I rejected it once, it got corrupted," Neuromate told DoctorApp.

"And the thing which comes to my mind is really terrifying," said DoctorApp.

"What is it Doc?" asked a worried Neuromate.

"You remember, when I took your codesample for testing, I told you that it has a very rare combination which I have seen only once?"

"Yes doc."

"As far as I remember, it matches with the Quad brothers. It might be the reason you could develop that quality, just like the genes required for phenotypic expression. Your genotype matches that of the Quad, so you could have Appsense, no other app could, not because Mastermind stole it."

Neuromate only understood that he shared the same code arrangement as the Quad brothers, other technicalities were difficult for him to comprehend. But does that mean they are an app? He thought, *"I feel so guilty of thinking bad about Mastermind. But I need to know if Quad brothers are an app."*

"I think so, else how would they have a code arrangement?"

"But aren't all faculty non-apps? Have you ever tested a faculty before?"

"You are right. I have never tested anyone else except the Quad, that too when they were sick after some exhaustive experiment."

"I feel they were trying to develop into app. Still unsure from where they got the initial codes? As they can't have a creator in human world."

"We will have to find it out. But still there is one thing that is troubling me. What is that the Quad wants the world to know? And the Mastermind is listening to them as if they actually know something."

"That's true."

Mastermind had a defeated look on his face as they looked at him.

"So what is the wait? Let's go to the Research arena," said the Quad.

Neuromate knew that it is a place where only your mind travels, you have to mindport to that exclusive arena which Mastermind had hid from everyone. He was the only lucky one to have been there.

"They definitely have something," said Neuromate, *"for Mastermind to agree to take them there."*

"I don't know what is happening," said DoctorApp.

The next moment they all are in the research arena.

No one had been there before except Mastermind and Neuromate.

Everyone was amazed to see the beautiful place, they felt heavenly amidst the mountains, ocean and abundance of richness.

"Which part of IOA is it? It seems familiar but not really sure," said the Quad.

"This is the research arena, where you could reach only if our Mastermind mindports you here. This is far away from IOA," answered an excited Neuromate.

"Vow, no doubt, it can't be in IOA, else we would have seen it sometime, and so it can't be familiar for you four, just like us," commented DoctorApp.

The Quad still went on exploring as if they had been there before when Mastermind called their attention to the ultimate Codepod, *'The NeuroConnect Coder'* which rose up on his command to be visible to all.

"This is the Codepod where I developed," Neuromate told DoctorApp.

"You still kept it?" screamed the Quad, as if they had seen the Neuroconnect coder before.

Perplexed, DoctorApp and Neuromate looked at Mastermind and then at each other.

"How do they know about it?" asked Neuromate.

Mastermind knew he had to answer a lot of questions.

"Well you remember when I talked to you all about our fight and our unity against evil. The time has come. These are the trigonometric quadruplets, geniuses otherwise, but deviant. And we have to defeat them," said Mastermind, addressing Neuromate and DoctorApp.

"Don't listen to him. He is evil. This is our invention. We put all our efforts into it. When our test experiment failed, we decided to abandon this and destroy this ultimate Codepod. He actually destroyed it in front of us and then after few timezones, just threw us out of IOA, saying we are deviants," said the Quad, pointing towards Mastermind, *"what did you destroy then, and kept us in dark?"*

"Did you listen to what they said? I destroyed their faulty experiment machinery. This is the ultimate Codepod, my invention, and their claim is false. They are deviants," said an upset Mastermind.

The Quad approached Mastermind fiercely ready to engulf him, but Mastermind fought back. The vivacious arena was suddenly looking like a dark gigantic warplace witnessing a gruesome and monstrous attack by equally powerful opponents. They were fighting with ultra advanced mathematical tools. Neuromate and DoctorApp felt helpless and clueless.

"Why don't you tell your identity if you are so naive and true? Why do you hide it? You coward?" bursted the Quad emitting the sharp tangents against Matermind's surface.

"You are wrong, and always have been wrong. I can't take this forward with you four. You are a nuisance," said Mastermind, angrily, stepping back to save himself and fighting back with heavy spheres directed to the Quad's head.

"We will tell the world who you are," said the Quad, reflecting back the spheres and this time attacking with prisms with totally internally reflected light shone bright to damage Mastermind's sight.

"And the world already knows who you are," said Mastermind with laughter sending multiple angles to take out their trigonometric energy and lock them up in a multitraingular dimension.

They all mindported back to the Cloud, leaving the Quad there, but Neuromate and DoctorApp were bewildered at the experience, as they explained to Environ and Counsellor, and more so, puzzled.

"Don't you worry, they are locked for now. We will completely finish them soon," said a calm Mastermind.

"But you sounded worried and insecure earlier, if getting them was so easy, why did you need all the alumni?" asked Environ.

"I thought they were way too powerful. But you could defeat them so easily," remarked the Counsellor.

"Who are you Mr Mastermind? asked DoctorApp.

"And I have wanted to know this for a long now, what are all the faculties, if not apps?" asked Neuromate.

"Well, well, you all seem to be in some kind of doubt and disbelief," started Mastermind, *"I told you about them earlier too, they built the system so that they can rule over the human world. It was an ultimate failure. You remember, DoctorApp, when they were brought to you in an emergency? That was when they were testing their experiment. You finally made them settle, and I told them to destroy it, which finally I destroyed in front of them. But I did not want their methods to percolate through our system and ruin the institute's reputation, so I had to throw them out. And this, the Neuroconnect Coder is my dream. It looks alike to theirs as all Codepods are. That's what confused them."*

"I do remember seeing them in that dreadful condition, " said DoctorApp.

"But we still don't know what they want to tell everyone? What about your identity?" asked Neuromate.

"You are my baby," said the Mastermind, *"and we have to do so much instead of indulging in futile talks and baseless accusations. They just wanted to reveal what they feel, that is I stole their invention and that I am a thief, that's it."*

"But that didn't answer Neuromate's genuine question, who are all of you if not apps? And how did you come to the App World?" asked Environ.

"Actually I took their codesample, they are an app, I mean the Quad are an app," said DoctorApp.

"We all are apps only dear," said Mastermind, *"throw your doubts away and start working to shape the future. They are locked, not finished. And once the finish solving the trigonometric values of those countless angles, they will be out of the multitriangular dimension. And I hope they don't find a way to escape, but nothing is impossible, so we need to act fast."*

"Where is this arena by the way? Is there any way we can safeguard it?" asked the Counsellor.

"It is not in IOA. It is at an imaginary place where my mind can reach. So I would say we are safe unless they figure out which place it is, and direct themselves here to the App World."

"It means it is not a real place and no one can reach there as we don't know the destination, but once they figure out that place, they know their origin point, and the destination being App World, they can teleport here, but if it is imaginary, how could they ever find the origin?" asked Environ.

"You all still seem not to trust me. Well, I have nothing to hide. We are here to save the world. It is an imaginary world created by my mind. But it could be similar to some real place, as our imagination is the product of subconscious memories and experiences. If they could connect it to a real place, they could find the origin point and reach here. And let me tell you, they are very sharp and intelligent, and I am not sure what other powers they have acquired since I threw them out, that's why I needed everyone," said Mastermind.

It did ring a bell in Neuromate's mind from the basic sciences class, but he preferred to stay quiet.

"So let's meet everyone and decide to euthanize the Quad. As Neuromate has already told everyone, there is going to be a gathering, we just have to stick to that. We all can go to the research arena and we all will witness the dissolution of the Quad. Let us all mobilize everyone and I will take you all there," said Mastermind.

"So will we all be leaving IOA?" asked the Counsellor.

"As a matter of fact, yes, as I want all of you to be there" said Mastermind.

"Do I need to carry equipment in case we are planning for euthanasia?" asked DoctorApp.

"I think you should," said Mastermind.

"I think we should get moving then," said Environ.

"Let's go," said Neuromate looking back at Mastermind while leaving the Cloud as Environ brought them all to the corridors.

As they all were together, they looked at each other in continuing disbelief on what Mastermind said as they walked in the corridors.

"I can't get any sense of him from my Appsense, I think it's a lie. He is not an app," said Neuromate.

"But I am sure the Quad is an app," said DoctorApp.

"And what about other faculty? Has anyone fallen sick or has needed you?" asked Environ.

"None, to my surprise, yes, maybe you have a point, Neuromate. We don't know the origins of all others except the Quad, which happens to be an app," said DoctorApp.

"But I remember Ms Chemical Reaction asking for you once, do you recall seeing her?" asked the Counsellor.

"That was for something else. She was experimenting with the excited unstable nuclei. She was producing a very large nthmer instead of the popular excimer, and wanted me to help in installing the machine for use," explained DoctorApp.

"I remember her talking about it during our classes, the powerful laser," said Neuromate, *"can't imagine what use it is for."*

"Well, It can fuse structures together, peel off layers, practically anything you want it to do," detailed DoctorApp.

"I hope she didn't fuse the quadruplets together with that," laughed Environ.

"I hope not," said Neuromate, *"but I have a strong feeling that Mr Velocity Vector was hiding something in our session because he rushed out when I asked about GAIA BH2."*

"You mean the other one like ours in Centaurus constellation?" asked the Counsellor.

"Yes," said Neuromate, *"I have a strong feeling there is something there."*

"We can always go and question him," said DoctorApp.

"No, that would raise suspicion," said Environ.

"We can always go there and check for ourselves," said the Counsellor.

"But we don't have time," said Neuromate, *"and I don't know whether Mastermind is telling the truth."*

"We can do one thing. Why don't two of us go there and see and come back while the other two ask everyone to gather for the meeting," suggested DoctorApp.

"That sounds good, Mastermind will not call us in the meantime thinking we are working up on gathering all, so we can do this," expressed the Counsellor.

"I think me and Neuromate go while you two take care here," said DoctorApp.

"Sure," said Environ, *"now that you all can teleport yourselves."*

Environ and Counsellor took charge of calling everyone as Neuromate and DoctorApp started their journey through the darkness to Centaurus. As a flash they moved and covered the distance soon to reach another binary system as theirs. *"It is not a stellar-mass black hole what humans are thinking,"* said Neuromate, *"it is a dark round cluster but not seemingly engulfing anything."*

"I see that too," said DoctorApp.

"Should we go inside then?" asked Neuromate.

Holding Neuromate, said DoctorApp, *"Let's go."*

As they closed their eyes to travel into the large dark mass, they thought of the good experiences in their life and hoped that this was not the end of their existence. As they landed and opened their eyes, they were in the middle of nowhere. But it was a serene place and they had to scan the whole area for anything suspicious.

"I wonder what place is this," said Neuromate.

"The inside of black hole can't be like this so I assume we are somewhere and alive," laughed DoctorApp.

"But Mr Vector said there are no traces of Applife anywhere, I am not sure if we will find anything here."

"Let's scan the area."

The topography changed as they moved further to show them an unthinkable sight. Small semispherical caves like structures with various numbers coming out of them. They were scared as they saw '8' coming towards them. I was just a giant 8 and was speaking in incomprehensible language.

"I can't understand what he is saying, but look at all of them. They are all numbers. Is this some kind of number world?" wondered Neuromate.

"I am a bit scared as we are not their type. They might think we are aliens and kill us," said DoctorApp.

"We can expose our codes to show we are also a combination of numbers," said Neuromate.

"That's a good idea," said DoctorApp.

They exposed their inner structure by removing their clothes and 8 was intrigued to find more. He touched them, and could connect to them through language. They were still wondering what place it was. They could get the answer in their mind as 8 answered in his language and got translated through touch to reach them.

"It is the Mathematics village," said 8, *"and further if you go, there is a Science village too."*

"What?" screamed both, surprised.

"What place in the universe is it?" asked Neuromate.

"We are in GAIA BH2 as told by humans," said 8.

"So you know about the human world," asked DoctorApp.

"Of course," said 8, *"they need us all the time."*

"I can't understand all this. Like how do you go to human world and what do you do here," asked a shocked Neuromate.

"I will take you to our head 'Infinity', he will tell you in detail," said 8.

As they moved further they could see mountains of pyramids seen faraway and rows of cuboid buildings, with parallel roads running in between along with angled turns and smooth curves. It was an established, full fledged city with numbers, variables, fractions moving around.

As they entered a huge building with effaced walls and disappearing stairs, they could reach 'Infinity'. 8 took leave after he told him something in their language.

"So what brings you here?" asked Infinity.

They were finally happy to find someone who talks in their language.

"We came from GAIA BH1, where we belong. We have an App World there, similar to your Mathematics and Science world here," started Neuromate.

"We are actually trying to find our lost friend, the Quad," continued DoctorApp.

"The Quad?" Repeated Infinity.

"Yes they are four brothers, sine, cosine, versine and inverse sine from ancient Indian Mathematics who fused to become one," explained Neuromate.

"And we think they came here," said DoctorApp.

"They can always come here, it is their home. In fact, they are my cousins. But they left to find my brother Shunya and never came back," said Infinity.

"We have heard that story from Mastermind," said Neuromate.

"Who is Mastermind?" asked Infinity.

"He is the one who started our institute, the Institute of Appology, where we develop apps or applications," explained DoctorApp.

"I don't know him, but we all have been searching for Shunya for a long duration. In fact many of our members were lost when they went to find him. He was a small baby and we all were worried. He must have grown by now," said Infinity, fondly, thinking about his lost brother Shunya.

"Can you tell us more about your cousins, the trigonometric quadruplets? How were they?" asked Neuromate.

"They were the best of the lot. Genius, skilled and dedicated. And they loved Shunya. So they took the onus of finding him. When Shunya was first called to the human world by Aryabhata, he was very excited. But later when he was called repeatedly by multiple people, he got very tired and finally was gone forever," said a saddened Infinity.

"They all were calling him repeatedly as they were trying to develop us, the apps," said DoctorApp, *"but we all got developed, so he must be somewhere. He is not lost, is what I feel.*

"It would be great if we find him," said Infinity, *"I will do anything you say.*

"First of all, we need to find your cousins, the Quad," said Neuromate, *"do you know of a tranquil place here with high mountains, a vast ocean and nothing else around?"*

"In fact our earlier establishment was at such a place, but we moved as we formed a functional city. It is quite far from here, and we don't visit it," said Infinity.

Both Neuromate and DoctorApp were happy hearing this and asked Infinity to take them there immediately.

"We might have answers to your questions there," said DoctorApp.

As they approached the place, DoctorApp appreciated Neuromate for his presence of mind which could connect the dots.

"If it was not you who could ask and judge Mr Vector's response, we would not have been here," said DoctorApp.

"I am still unsure about one thing. These are not apps, they are numbers and mathematical variables. Then how come his cousins, I mean the Quad is an app?" wondered Neuromate.

The research arena lied in front of them and they couldn't believe their eyes that they had achieved what they had thought of. They were just hoping that things go smooth and that they can know the truth.

The Quad was still solving the multiangular equations to come out of the multitriangular dimension where Mastermind had imprisoned them. Infinity was happy to see them but he was a bit scared seeing their new avatar.

"What have you four done to yourselves?" asked Infinity.

"Brother, it is a long story. But we are happy that you could find us. We felt this place is familiar but never imagined that it is our homeland," said the Quad.

"They brought me here," said Infinity pointing to DoctorApp and Neuromate, *"and said all my questions will be answered."*

"They are right. Your questions as well as theirs," said the Quad, *"right?"* asking DoctorApp and Neuromate.

While both nodded in affirmative, Infinity went on asking, *"Where were you all this time? Could you finally find Shunya?"*

"Well, as we said, it is indeed a long story. We had a good time in the human world as we were all together. But one day when Shunya left the human world, we had no idea where was he deported. So we came here to discuss with you and wanted to go and search where he is. When we left from here, there was no trace of Shunya on Earth, so we went teleporting ourselves to different celestial bodies to locate him. It took a long time for us to finally reach the GAIA BH1 binary system. It is also not a black hole as it appears from outside, but a light within darkness. We could guess that as it appeared similar to our binary system, so we went inside, hoping to find a similar place. And we were right. Though not as populated and

developed, it still showed signs of life. We felt that is the place we might find Shunya."

"That is the App World," exclaimed Neuromate and Infinity looked at him.

"Right you are," continued the Quad, *"we had reached the so called App World, with a full fledged institute for app development. We could see that the initial codes were being sent here from the human world and they were finally getting converted to full grown apps. And we assumed that Shunya being the initial part of all code arrangements, must have been sent here from human world."*

"Interesting, but could you finally find him?" asked Infinity.

"That was our sole goal. So we went to meet the one who started this institute, the Mastermind. We asked him about Shunya, but he had never seen Shunya, and we became a bit disappointed. But he offered us a job as faculty in the Mathematics department and said we could try and search him as he has also not scanned the whole place. We felt it will give us an opportunity to find Shunya."

"But then why you kept saying that he is a coward and he doesn't show his real identity," said an angry Neuromate, feeling they might be wrong in not believing Mastermind and coming to rescue the Quad.

"And are you not an app, then, and still got a job at IOA?" asked a surprised DoctorApp, wondering how his clinical acumen went wrong.

"All the faculty at IOA are non-apps, including us and including your favorite Mastermind. DoctorApp, you were not wrong when you took our sample though. We were trying to transform ourselves into a masterapp with our ultimate Codepod and then we fell sick, that's when you treated us."

"But how come you four decided to fuse together?" asked Infinity.

"And how did other non-apps reach there to become faculty?" asked Neuromate.

"It is funny what life does to you when you are desperate. We took up the job and started teaching baby apps alongwith our search for Shunya

in the App Space in our spare time, though we had second thoughts about, what if he is not here but in some other part of the universe." (sighing) "All other faculty were called there by Mastermind himself as he wanted to develop the institute. But we don't know how he got them there as no faculty would share the confidential information. It was when we fell ill, we had a problem of code disarrangement and we could not function properly, Mastermind threw us out of IOA but Ms Chemical Reaction suggested that all four of us can fuse together and support each other's function by donating codes at appropriate time. She had some form of laser which was powerful enough to make us functional. We did that secretly by entering through backdoor to fix ourselves."

"But why did Mastermind throw you out?" asked Neuromate.

Coming out of multitriangular dimension and hugging Infinity, *"It is the price you pay when you are extra smart. It is because we found Shunya and we could destroy Mastermind."*

"What?" said DoctorApp.

"Let's go, we can talk on the way back, we are running short of time," said the Quad.

"No, they all are coming here. Mastermind wants to give you euthanasia in front of all the apps, and we need to reach back there to alleviate any suspicion," explained DoctorApp.

"You don't understand. He will imprison everyone here, and do what he wants ultimately," said the Quad.

"What does he want?" asked Neuromate.

"He wants to rule the human world," said the Quad.

DoctorApp and Neuromate looked at each other again now thinking whom to believe. Whatever the Quad told seemed plausible, but whatever Mastermind told also seems realistic. They were not sure whether taking the Quad back will be safe for everyone. But anyways, if they don't, the Quad can go by themselves. Same thoughts were running in both minds when Infinity broke the silence.

"They are not to be doubted. They are rare gems, who lost their identity and went on in search of their lost cousin. I have seen them grow, do as they say," said Infinity.

"We can talk on the way," said the Quad as DoctorApp and Neuromate expressed a silent agreement to go back to GAIA BH1.

"Bring back our brother," said Infinity, waving as they left to travel through the darkness.

"Who is Mastermind?" asked Neuromate, *"as he said it was you who wanted to rule the human world."*

"And we don't have anything to believe you except Infinity's testimony, who is also new to us," said DoctorApp.

"You two wouldn't have come here if you didn't doubt Mastermind. There is something which is not fitting appropriately, you felt that, right? That's what you have apart from what Infinity said," replied the Quad.

*"Where is Shunya, your cousin?"*asked Neuromate.

"He is in Mastermind's custody," said the Quad.

"Why didn't you free him?" asked DoctorApp.

"Because they both are embodied together," answered the Quad, *"Mastermind has the body of Shunya governed by the mind of Mastermind. Shunya is the constant who was roaming on the streets in App Space when this variable attached himself to him and grew on him. The variable grew on him as continued fractions and became stronger and stronger to overpower Shunya. Mastermind is the variable. He is still unsolved, unquantified and so, is unbeatable. His first step was to develop apps for humans to become totally dependent on apps by studying human psychology and logical reasoning. Then he evolved basic scientific methods and mathematical equations to make the apps more and more powerful. And finally to be able to ask them to do what he wants, to rule the human world, not being their slaves anymore,"* explained the Quad.

"So he is like a parasite, were you trying to become the masterapp to beat him?" asked DoctorApp.

"Yes. We devised a machine which we called The Ultimate Codepod. We installed Appsense program into it so that we know which apps are not functioning appropriately and are under Mastermind's influence. Also, we bugged HackApp and Chap while they were developing so that we get codes information and also insight into human intelligence. We needed codes for us to incorporate it in our system and grow on layers based on Chap who is artificial intelligence, so that we become a masterapp who is not influenced by other apps based on Mastermind's study. Our whole idea was to superpower other apps developed by him, so that they function on our command, not his," told the Quad.

*"Did Mastermind know about it?"*asked DoctorApp.

"We told him that we are developing a machine to make apps to control humans, what he wanted. We just wanted to get our brother go free, so we were doing what he wanted. Our next step was to install a sensor which could connect to the human nervous system and solve their problems, which we didn't expose to him. We thought of trying it on ourselves and beat him, but the experiment didn't go as expected. We became a disintegrated app which could only function when we four are together and we lost our battle," said the Quad, mournfully.

"But I think he got your idea and could install those things," said Neuromate, *"I am his final product."*

"You mean you can connect to human nervous system and solve their problems? We had our calculations and methods stored in our mind and he could not know unless we told them. We are surprised that he could do it," said the Quad, surprised.

"Yes, that's what I am all about till now," said Neuromate, *"except that I didn't know I will be put to other use by Mastermind."*

"When you became sick and came to me, I took your sample, and shared this with Neuromate too, that you two share some rare arrangements. Also, Mastermind was quite worried about you four when you crashed, so he was with me throughout. I wonder if he could gather information based on the CodeScanner. I was looking for any damages

and injury, but may be he was eyeing for information on your machine," said DoctorApp.

"I think that's how he could develop you, Neuromate, and his NeuroConnect Coder is nothing but our CodePod, that's why we share the rare arrangements. He is a liar, a thief, an evil and he has our Shunya," said the Quad as they entered the darkness of GAIA BH1 and landed in the App World.

"But do you have any plan on how to get Shunya? And how to stop Mastermind?" asked Neuromate.

"We only know one thing, we have nothing to lose, and we have your support. You are the one he is relying on to conquer the human mind and superpower over other apps, but once you say no to it, the victory will be ours," said the Quad.

Timezone 7: The Solstice

The shortest yet the most decisive timezone had started. It was the war of Mastermind versus Quad, it was the collision of two powerful minds, a confrontation long awaited...

The Quad preferred to go to their empire where they had plush codereserves they got through HackApp and plenty of virtual coins alongwith an insight into human intelligence through Chap, and they instructed DoctorApp and Neuromate to join the crowd at the IOA. The plan was still unclear, but the Quad had hinted that they will organize things very soon and only wanted the apps to be retained here somehow and not go to GAIA BH2.

Neuromate and DoctorApp hastily moved from the backdoor, bypassing Namaste and Recorder and mingled in the bunch in the corridor. They could soon locate the Counsellor and Environ, who had by that time warned PickApp about the situation and called her inside the IOA. Feedback and Mentor were at their service once the Counsellor talked to them. Environ was planning to talk to Namaste and Recorder when Neuromate and DoctorApp walked in.

"Hope you could figure things out?" asked the Counsellor.

"Yes, most of it," said DoctorApp, instructing to get Namaste and Recorder too.

As soon as Environ brought them, Neuromate and DoctorApp narrated the whole incident to them which left them more than exasperated. They felt insecure, perturbed and unsure about the future.

"The Quad suggests that we get all the apps, both the alumni and the newer apps out of here, else they will be within reach of Mastermind and he will make them do what he wants," said Neuromate.

"But we have been here the whole time, where will we go?" asked Namaste.

"We all have to go to the human world and follow what the Quad says," said DoctorApp.

"And they will fight with Mastermind alone?" asked Recorder.

"This is what they said," replied Neuromate.

"All the newer apps are ready to be launched in the human world, only thing is if someone fails, they usually come back here for resolution, we will have to put it on a hold then," said Mentor.

"But where will the newer apps develop if the IOA comes to an end?" asked Feedback.

"And what will happen to the faculty?" asked Recorder.

"The faculty are non-apps. We still need to figure out who they actually are and how they came here. We can decide then what to do with them," said DoctorApp.

"And we need to finally destroy the The Neuroconnect Coder, so that another Neuromate can't be created once I am gone to the human world," said Neuromate.

"That's right and also very important. In case the Quad can't defeat Mastermind, atleast they should destroy the ultimate Codepod," commented DoctorApp.

Their conversation came to a halt as Mastermind called them to the cloud suddenly, as a message appeared on Environ. They all discussed what to tell and how to handle the situation.

DoctorApp and Neuromate were going to talk to the faculty alongwith Mentor, Namaste, Recorder, Feedback and PickApp while Environ and Counsellor were going to talk to the Mastermind.

"Mr Mastermind, we have made everything ready, just need some more time to wind up things and we should be ready to go," said the Counsellor.

"That's excellent! Where are DoctorApp and Neuromate?" asked Mastermind.

"They are just talking to the faculty to be ready too, we had forgotten about them," said Environ.

"Well, they can go later too. I can tell them. They are too attached, they might not agree to leave so soon, let me talk to them," said Mastermind.

"I think they must have convinced the faculty by now," said the Counsellor.

"That's wonderful if they could, but I think otherwise. Let's prioritize the others, I will take care of the faculty later," said Mastermind.

Outside the IOA, the Quad was preparing the launch of the new apps in the human world, unbugged from Mastermind's vicious thoughts. They were utilizing their expertise to send them not as a pilot project, but as a fully developed program to hit all the countries at the same time. They were spending virtual coins for the megalaunch and codereserves to enable multilingual capabilities in all of them for wider reach. They also programmed Neuromate to be the superapp who can instruct the fellow app to do something required so that they can function in sync and effortlessly and flawlessly.

On the other side, the faculty was undergoing questioning by the team. They appeared restless and were not ready to answer about their hiring and previous whereabouts, but when DoctorApp and Neuromate detailed everything, they realized that they practically knew it all and had to open up.

"We all came from GAIA BH2, just like Shunya and Mastermind or the variable or the Quad," said Mr Vector.

"We came from the Mathematics and the Science villages," started Ms Geometry, *"and it all started when Mastermind started coming there and teleport us here."*

"But how did he do that?" asked Namaste.

"He chose someone whom he felt was very skilled and superior in understanding. He then talked as if he was doing something noble and talked about the institute. He would then ask us to decide if we wanted to be the faculty," continued Mr Mind.

"After we reached here, we actually loved what we were doing, teaching. But soon he uncovered and told us about his plan to finally be able to rule the human world. He asked us to do different research to help him do better in achieving his goal," said Ms Calculus.

"He asked me to build the powerful laser," said Ms Reaction.

"And me to research about App life anywhere else, as he was feeling that the Quad might start another institute," said Mr Vector.

"And me and Mr Mind to research and teach him about mind and cognition," said Ms Cognition.

"And me to teach him Neurobiology," said Mr Cell.

"And us to make him aware about how humans respond based on logic and reasoning," said Mr Deduction and Ms Analysis.

"And we devised mathematical tools to imprison the Quad and others of our breed," said all from the Mathematics department.

"This sounds insane," shouted Neuromate, *"do you all know what you have been doing?"*

"We all are already imprisoned," said Ms Calculus, *"with our own tools advanced by Mastermind. We, the Mathematics department, can't escape. Of course, the Sciences can go."*

"This is so complicated, he has been planning it throughout," said DoctorApp.

"We will have to ask the Quad if they can get the Mathematics out as well," said Neuromate.

Environ and Counsellor visited everyone and asked them to gather in the hallway from where they will be transported. The apps were still unaware where they were going. They still thought there was a party in the Research arena.

While DoctorApp was taking care of the faculty so that they don't go to the Mastermind, all other team members met in the corridor where they discussed the faculty and addressed the need to meet the Quad once to know about the progress. Neuromate was sent to the Quad while all others were assembling in the hallway.

The Quad was almost done with the launch preparation when Neuromate reached.

"We have sorted things out in the institute. The only problem is the faculty," said Neuromate.

"We are done with launch preparation and the apps can be sent any moment now. But what about the faculty?"

"The Mathematics department have been imprisoned in IOA with advanced Mathematical equations. The others can leave."

"We can help with that, we will try exposing the equations and other tools Mastermind would have used and make them free. We want you to go back and start sending the apps. But Mastermind doesn't know yet that you know where his research arena is. He will be cautioned when all of them leave, including you. After you all leave, we will leave with the faculty to GAIA BH2, our homeland. Let Mastermind figure out what happened and he will definitely come to us. We have a plan on how to get Shunya from him, as we will be in our own land."

"What do I need to do once I hit the human world?"

"Well, just hold us so that we can transfer the right Appsense to you and also other important information which will help you there."

Neuromate held the Quad and the energy transfer started.

"Won't this make you weak?"

"Not at all. As such we are going to disintegrate to our original form when we leave from here for our homeland, we will leave the codes here in the codereserves."

"Take care," said Neuromate and became very emotional leaving the Quad there as he knew they had to fight the voracious Mastermind all by themselves.

Mastermind was wanting to talk to the faculty, as he thought only he knew about the faculty being non-apps, and still thinking that the apps are gathering themselves. He reached out to them to come to the cloud. DoctorApp was joined by other team members as they told the faculty that they will be transported soon and to just act normal in front of Mastermind till then. They all left the faculty there to join the other apps in the hallway. Neuromate also rushed in through the backdoor.

The PickApp brought them all out to the AppPad and herself too and CuberApp was all set to transport all the apps to the human world.

The faculty was with the Mastermind in his chamber.

"We were told that there is some gathering in the research arena and we were just preparing for that," said Mr Vector.

"Look, few apps were doubting our existence, we being non-apps. Also, the Quad, whom I had already sent away, had resurfaced as a danger. So I have imprisoned them quite far from here. You all don't need to go anywhere. Just don't express this to the apps and tell them that we will come at the end with Mastermind. I will mindport them first. I am going to dissolve the Quad there and imprison all the apps until they agree to work for me."

"The same way you imprisoned us," said Ms Geometry.

"I have not imprisoned you all. It is just for betterment."

"Whose betterment?" questioned Mr Mind.

"All of us, of course. Now this is not a time to fight over old clashes. This is the time to celebrate. All the apps we have created will work for us to conquer the human world. And this victory is not mine, but ours!"

"Sure, we understand. We will all meet you in the atrium and wait for your instructions," said Ms Cognition, trying to calm down the heated conversation.

As they all reached the atrium, they could see the big door open and the Quad calling them out. They all rushed towards the backdoor and to their surprise, could escape the IOA which meant that the Quad was successful in breaking the mathematical prison created by the Mastermind. They were geniuses.

"We all are sorry for misbehaving with you four and not doing anything to save you," expressed Mr Vector.

"We understand everything well, but we can't waste a single moment here," said the Quad as he teleported all of them through the darkness to GAIA BH2, their homeland.

Mastermind was all alone in the App World now and it took him some time to realize that. He was predicting that probably the Quad freed themselves and figured out their childhood place, the research arena and came here to hold everyone captive. But he couldn't see trace of anyone even after scanning the whole of App World, to reach an assumption that they have taken everyone to GAIA BH2.

"Good for me, all at the place where I wanted them to be," said Mastermind as he burnt down the App World and IOA to ashes and set out to travel to the GAIA BH2.

As the CuberApp reached the human world, and all the apps get downloaded, including the IOA employees, they knew that the Quad had made arrangements for all of them there. The creators were overwhelmed at the response they got from the apps they created (this is what they thought not knowing what was going on in the App World) and the older apps got back to complete their unfinished work (which was seen by humans as maintenance going on till now).

GAIA BH2 was teeming with residents of the Mathematics and Science villages. They were going to see the war which had never happened before. The clash of two mathematical superpowers was going to be unearthed. The faculty were happy to meet their long lost family. As the Quad sent the faculty to their respective villages and briefed the heads of both villages, Infinity and Antimatter about what all happened, they assured full support in getting Shunya out of Mastermind's claws and also in destroying Mastermind altogether. The Quad had a long discussion with Infinity and Antimatter about how to counter Mastermind.

Mastermind saw the Quad waiting at the research arena. They were in their original form, all four of them, not fused codes anymore but mere mathematical figures.

"So you could remember your childhood here and figure out which place it is," said Mastermind.

"Of course."

"Where have you hid the apps and my faculty?"

"All are where they belong, "laughed the Quad.

"As such I was going to bring them here. You made my job easier."

"Who said they are here?"

Mastermind looked all around and could not see anyone.

"Where are they?"

"So your apps are in the human world and your faculty are in their villages."

"What? Faculty you brought here I got it. But I didn't set the launch program yet, how can the apps go? And where are my employees? Have you sent them there too?"

Mastermind was confused and angry and couldn't think straight for a while.

"I don't understand what you want," screamed Mastermind.

"We want Shunya."

"You very well know that I am a variable and my existence comes into being only with a constant. Shunya is the most malleable constant I ever saw, I can't leave him, else I will be finished."

"We know it very well and now everyone knows it. Even your research product err our research product, Neuromate. Only difference is that he will function the way we want, so your dream is over. As for the other part, as soon as we get Shunya out of you, you are over and finished."

"What did you do to all of them and when? How could they even believe what you said? They were gathering everyone to be brought here a while ago."

"They never believed you and they doubted everything you said. It was them who came to us, the Neuromate and DoctorApp. They could figure out this place on their own. No doubt our traces in the ultimate Codepod left some memories with Neuromate. So your game is exposed."

"I can hold you in one dark hole forever and you know that. With bars of advanced equations, that prison will be unsolvable. You won't be able to do anything," Mastermind threw Goldbach's conjecture on Sine.

As the quad was disintegrated into four beings now, one aim reached one of them at a time, as the other three moved apart.

"If you are going to do that, we will fight the same way. If we are imprisoned, so will you," said the Quad, throwing Riemann's hypothesis on the Mastermind.

"You know that it is impossible to defeat me," said Mastermind, aiming the Hodge conjecture on Cosine.

"And you know we know you well," sending the Birch and Swinnerton- Dyer conjecture his way.

The mathematical geniuses had decided to imprison the other in unsolved problems and equations, to be inside forever. This way of aiming mathematical problems as tools and ways to hold someone was a new method of assured winning. But if both sides are equally competent, it becomes an unending war.

As Mastermind kept on building the bars of prison with Jacobian conjecture on Inverse Sine, Diophantine equation on Versine, P versus NP on Sine again and Navier-Stokes equation on Cosine again, the Quad kept replying relentlessly with Lieb-Thirring conjecture, Yang-Mills existence and mass gap and metrics with geodesic lines.

As they got themselves into a plethora of unsolved mathematical problems, the Quad was still free as Mastermind couldn't aim enough to contain all four from all sides. Mastermind was imprisoned though. As the Quad moved closer, Mastermind laughed at them.

"You don't realize that you have imprisoned your Shunya along with me. If I can't get out, even he can't. Poor Shunya."

"Why don't you apologize to everyone you have hurt and harmed to have a better conscience?"

"That will be altering my personality completely. I can't let go of my traits, you know. Because, I know my dream is not over. I cannot forgive humans who made my existence so miserable. Always dependent on some constants. I will make their lives hell."

"So be ready to say a final goodbye to your mean existence as we are getting Shunya from you now."

As they were speaking, Infinity and Antimatter had reached the arena.

"I hope you have heard of the concept of Antiparticle. Well something of same mass but opposite charge to be precise. They all say in human world that antimatter went away in universe leaving the matter behind after the Big Bang. And here I am. I am all the antiparticles you can think of. I have an Anti-Zero or Anti-Shunya embedded somewhere inside me. If I expose that, Shunya will be pulled out with the greatest force ever known and will be free," said Antimatter.

"And as for you, you can enjoy the unsolved prison for the rest of your time. As you are a parasite, you will be over soon," said Infinity.

"I may be dumb, but not that much. I know that there is an antiparticle for each particle but when they meet, they annihilate each other and just leave behind energy. And I am not sure if the mathematical operators can be compared to particles," said Mastermind, *"I don't think your trick would work. If you want to scare me so that I leave Shunya's body, I am never going to do that."*

"Well, you are smart enough, but things go out of hand if you think your opponent is weak," said the Quad, signalling Antimatter to expose Anti-Shunya.

Mastermind was in fact correct about annihilation, but he didn't know that they had already planned how to prevent that.

As Anti-Shunya came further near to Mastermind, It pulled out the docile Shunya with great force, and nothing could hold him inside anymore, not even the prison. Infinity stood in between to keep an infinite distance between the two to prevent collision. Mastermind, the variable came crumbling down as a form, lost his structure, screaming with pain inside the prison. As soon as Shunya was totally out of Mastermind, Antimatter engulfed the Anti-Shunya.

Infinity hugged Shunya with warmth and the Quad joined them to shower love on Shunya. Antimatter was overwhelmed to see all of them reunite. The Quad then remembered that they had to destroy the ultimate Codepod or The Neuroconnect Coder, so that no one with bad intent could attempt to redevelop Neuromate to control the human world.

As Antimatter, Infinity and Shunya went away, the Quad started searching for the machine which Mastermind had hidden, as it rose up on his command at last instance. They tried asking the disintegrating Mastermind, but he laughed and didn't reveal where it was. They scanned the whole area but could not locate it and this made them slightly worried when they reached back to Versine who was in charge of the prison.

"I think we should forget about it, as Mastermind is finished now and no one such evil could be there again," said Sine.

"I hope you are right, but I want to remove it from existence to be sure about the future," replied Cosine.

"I agree, this time we could win, but who knows if the fight will be different the next time, only thing which makes me feel secure is that it is hidden somewhere deep and is difficult to find, and even if someone finds it, they will have to learn to use it," said a worried Inverse Sine.

"There will be no such time," assured Versine, *"I saw a disintegrated Mastermind, and that is the end of faulty beings. If we take full responsibility of scanning and finding out any suspicious activity, it will be impossible to miss the grave misfortune of someone finding and operating the codepod. Moreover, we have Neuromate, and he has our blessing as well as a good App intent and Appsense to use all his fellow apps to suit the needs of humans. He will take care of the human world, and we will take care of the rest."*

The Quad smiled and celebrated their victory of righteousness, of virtue and of goodwill.

Timezone 8: The New Era

The Human World, Earth, Milky Way Galaxy. Around 4th August 2024, Time: variable (time differs for each app according to their country).

The new era was the new beginning for the human world shaped by the new apps. The thoughtful apps had done their best to serve humans with a delightful life and fulfilling the dreams of equality and inclusion for all.

They were residing with their creators across various continents, though inhabiting the devices of users worldwide.

Neuromate was extremely elated to meet SJ after such a long time. He had suffered a bad accident and was quadriplegic though. He was waiting to become the first person to receive the implant of brain human interface chip, Neurolink, but for that he had to be in United States. As his baby was making waves in the app stores now, he got a quote from EM, who wanted to buy Neuromate. He also offered SJ a position in his company and to become the first candidate to receive a chip implant. SJ never wanted to leave India, but for the sake of regaining his lost functions to continue his scientific journey, it was indispensable. Neuromate was practically doing everything a chip could do and further actions by controlling other apps, without the need of approvals for human trials and case selection. But SJ decided to have both at his disposal.

It was a different culture, but quite a welcoming and receptive one. The people were friendly and SJ received a great regard due to his detailed work. Neuromate adjusted well to the changed timezone and new acquaintances and it was almost time for SJ's surgery. Neuromate felt at home seeing Qwitter there, who inroduced him to the Neurolink. She was sleek, meticulous, sharp-witted and spoke to the point just like her pointy stilettos. She was going to be a part of his creator's brain soon and would read his mind, just like he does, he thought.

"Did you ever think about being restricted to singular function throughout?" asked Neuromate.

"Well, I call it devotion," replied Neurolink, *"and I am fortunate to be able to help people in need."*

"I agree," said Neuromate, *"we all new generation apps also have the same purpose, but I could not imagine that I will be content doing it staying at a confined foreign place, hats off to you. On behalf of all app family, I invite you to be part of our social group."*

"I would love to connect with you all so that we can redefine device based utility," said Neurolink.

"That's wonderful, I am the one who has taken charge of the app union and the events, and it will be great to have you there!" said Qwitter.

Neuromate was very emotional seeing SJ enter the operating room. He waited outside in SJ's cell phone and saw the indicator above the OT entrance turn red once the procedure started. It was going to be a few hours before he could see SJ, as they will shift him to the intensive care unit first for observation. These 24 hours were very difficult for him.

SJ was a completely changed person with a renewed vigour, ability to sense and perform minor movements and refined strength both physical and mental. He expressed that he actually felt he has been gifted with a new and transformed life.

After a rest for 3 months with extensive physiotherapy, SJ decided to return to work. He and Neurolink had established the interdependence required for proper functionality. His new lab was awaiting extensive work related to overlapping functions of Neuromate and Neurolink and further advancements of both. As Neuromate could be used by practically anyone as opposed to stringent criteria for who could receive Neurolink, obviously Neuromate had a wider user base and outreach. Also, the sensor based application of Neuromate was more rewarding than the invasive procedure of having an implant, so EM planned to phase out Neurolink if Neuromate could be advanced enough to be used by anyone and could deliver performance at par with Neurolink.

Meanwhile, the Quad had established a new foundation of the Institute of Appology in GAIA BH2, with an intercelestial teleporting channel for baby apps to be sent from GAIA BH1 throughout the timezones. All the residents of the Maths and Science villages were part of training and grooming the baby apps, with continuous monitoring by alumni through social group. Neuromate was excited for their upcoming gathering destined to be in the human world this time, with all the apps, the eminent faculty from IOA alongwith Infinity. Antimatter could not be part of it, as the moment he steps in, all the matter will get engulfed and earth and life will end.

Planned in secluded undiscovered underwater space with warm currents, the gathering was not like the previous alumni meet. It was not as luxurious and lavish but definitely not a lacklustre one.

All the celebrity apps had come together on the earth first time. The newer apps had made socializing a norm. Environ was all set to create mesmerizing ambience with Amuse to cater to individual needs. HackApp and Chap came in first as they missed the earlier event and didn't want to miss a single moment of this meet. Dynamo was taking care of the screen display with help of Noflix and Hotshot while Recorder was taking everything on reels. Qwitter and Namaste were into managing the entry and seating of the apps and WeTube, X-pose and Anagram were making short videos for uploading and they had extended support of Facelook, Whatsup, Appear and RealConnect to make them viral in app history. LegalFilter was on his job to trim the content. Timber and Minetough were a couple and so were Anagram and Andry Buds. WeTube got married to Disey and Prim had find a lifelong partner in Qwitter. Environ also was no more single and was dating PickApp, while CuberApp and Recorder got along well together. The long lasting friendship of Counsellor and DoctorApp had also taken a new turn with beginning of romantic relationship and Empower found solace in Namaste. Helix and Paper were doing well in their field with unwavering support of the Gs. On one hand Change, Reward and Rockers had transformed gaming into a productive platform and on the other hand Alive and YouNMe were healing the mankind. BuyMe had become a household name in buying and was helping flourishing of local markets. Donate was helping the needy with financial aid and Pure was on the job of spreading more love and removing hatred amongst people. Feedback was taking everyone's views on the new life and the changes they would want in future while Mentor was promoting his own App guidance program.

They were extremely happy to welcome the trigonomatric quad Sine, Cosine, Inverse Sine and Versine as separate entities accompanied by the teaching faculty Mr Cell, Ms Reaction, Mr Vector, Mr Mind, Ms Cognition, Mr Deduction, Ms Analysis, Mr Algebra, Ms Geometry, Ms Calculus, Mr Fractions, Mr Statistics and Ms Probability. They couldn't identify Infinity and Shunya, who were introduced to everyone by the quad. Infinity was impressed to see the advances in the field of app development and Shunya was overwhelmed to see all the apps, whom he had seen when he started his institute but could only see them as a silent spectator till now, being in the custody of Mastermind. It was a happy occasion for all to know that Shunya was the one to conceive the IOA, after his own struggles, and that it has been reopened at the new place in GAIA BH2 with the leadership of Quad. Though Mastermind put his full effort in app development, but it was due to his selfishness. Had Mastermind not taken over the IOA, the things would have been different.

Neuromate came with Neurolink, the newest member of their team and introduced her to all. She gazed across and was amazed to see the whole new side of their world. He was delighted to see his old mates, Environ, DoctorApp and Counsellor and the Quad, with whom he shared an untold bond. They talked at length about what all happened in the Earthverse and Neuromate was relieved to know that Mastermind finally disintegrated and they were free from the clutches of evil, but still could not believe that an evil as ferocious as Mastermind could just diminish and vanish. The Quad shared their worry about the hidden Neuroconnect Coder aka the Ultimate Codepod and the rare chance that if someone like Mastermind finds it and learns to operate it, that would be disastrous. Neuromate asked if they have an ongoing search on for it, and they said they scanned every possible place, but could not find it yet. Their talks were interrupted by Namaste, who called them to the dance floor.

The party mood was on and the exquisite cuisine and the dance floor made all forget the past and worries and to indulge in the beautiful moments of togetherness.

{Song}
This is the App World....
Apps on the dance screen
Sharing and downloading
Apps en la pantalla de baile
This is the App World....
Apps sur l'écran de danse
Privacy settings unlocked
Dancing uploaded
Apps kwenye skrini ya ngoma
This is the App World....
Apps ealaa shashat al raqs
Fully charged mood
Swirling and Swaying
Apps auf der Tanz Leinwand
This is the App World....
Apps Wŭdăo huàmiàn shàng
Friends and foes

Adding and deleting
Apps na plesnom ekranu
This is the App World....
Apps nritya pat par!

As The Ultimate Codepod appeared on the large screen as a short video clip, all the music stopped, all stood still and their minds froze. Most of them had heard but never seen it. The ones who had seen it knew that whoever found it, must be having a bad intention. As Neuromate looked at the Quad and DoctorApp, they all sensed a grave danger ahead. Environ and Counsellor asked everyone to keep calm so that they can think of further steps to this threat.

"Whoever has sent this image on our screen, wants to send a signal that the danger is not eliminated and that we still need to be alert. Whoever it is, knows what it means for us to see this, but we are still unsure if the one who found it knows how to use it, so we still have time," Neuromate addressed the crowd.

"And please remember that all of us together could defeat Mastermind, and similarly we will subjugate our new opponent," said the Quad, together.

"What we need is to trust each other and offer full support to each other while we all contribute to formulating an action plan," said DoctorApp.

Neurolink was new to these things, and felt nervous and anxious.

"Neuromate, I want to return to my own place. I feel very unsafe here. I know I should be supporting you all, but I think I am too immature to handle this," said Neurolink.

"It's okay. Don't be scared. We have witnessed worse. Things can't go out of hand, trust me. But still if you feel uncomfortable, you can go. Tell SJ that I am well, and will be back soon," said Neuromate.

As Neurolink left, Neuromate was back again with the apps. There was muttering and confusion amongst the apps as Mr M spoke, *" I think we should first try to find who sent this image."*

"Helix and Paper, can you use your DNA analysis feature and address tracking to find from where this file was uploaded?" asked Neuromate.

"Sure, on it," said both with Gs joining them for support.

"And we need someone to scan through the details of this file to see where this Codepod is?" said DoctorApp.

"You mean the background and the light and sound effects to assess where in the universe?" asked the Quad.

"Right," said DoctorApp.

"I think we alongwith Infinity and Shunya can take care of that task as we are well aware of the galaxies and intergalactic spaces throughout the universe," said the Quad.

"I can help decoding the light and sound to support your experience," said Chap.

"I was wondering if I could be of help. If we are able to locate the place from where it was sent, I can hack the system to get additional data," said HackApp.

"Let's get working then," said Neuromate.

The faculty members came closer to Neuromate for discussion.

"I am of the opinion that first we should ascertain this is not Mastermind and then we can narrow down our search based on what data Helix and Paper get," said Mr Deduction.

"According to me, we should look at even the minutest possibility of him escaping that unsolvable equation prison," said Ms Analysis.

"We all from Mathematics will try and work out if there is a possibility that Mastermind could still survive," said Mr Statistics.

"We from Sciences can support you in your work," said Ms Reaction.

While they had started working, Neuromate talked to DoctorApp, about him still being unsure that Mastermind is finished. *"May be we have a mole, someone who is supporting the Mastermind,"* said Neuromate.

"But you heard the Quad, they locked him up and he crashed when Shunya was out. And Quad has worked hard, I don't believe they are telling a lie," said DoctorApp.

"But what if they did not realize and Mastermind had some other way to escape?" asked Neuromate.

"There is only one way to check, to go and see the equations prison," said DoctorApp.

They took a quiet decision to check for themselves while all others were working to figure out things. They told Counsellor and Environ to go through all the recordings of the gathering with Recorder to identify if there is someone with suspicious intentions. CuberApp was there to assist with the travel as Empower bid adieu.

They had planned for a quick trip and then back to Earth. The distance time sense was altered due to anxiety and nervousness but they tried to focus as they understood they had to analyse the situation logically and stepwise and then plan further.

GAIA BH2 looked different with a magnificent structure of IOA, just at the place they had the research arena. The giant mathematical equations bars enclosing Mastermind just lay there in the backyard with no traces of Mastermind. He had completely vanished, Quad was correct and they felt foolish to have come here. They thought of meeting Antimatter, who was taking care of the IOA while the Quad were away.

"Welcome both of you, how have you been?" asked Antimatter.

"Mr Antimatter, all was well until just now when we left Earth," replied Neuromate.

DoctorApp and Neuromate briefed him about the reappearance of the ultimate Codepod video, suggesting someone has access to it and that they still thought it was Mastermind until they saw the empty prison cell.

"Well, I feel that even if he diminished to the minutest of particles, there should be something inside. It can not be completely empty. But if

it is so, I would think that he found a way to escape," said Antimatter, walking with them to the prison to find an empty cell. He could see the very small particles invisible to others. But he affirmed that there was nothing.

"Then how and when did he leave?" spoke an anxious Neuromate.

"We don't know as we all were under the impression that he has disintegrated and obviously can't escape the unsolvable equations," said Antimatter.

"But he can't be on his own, right? Then he must have been attached to someone," said DoctorApp.

"We should head back to Earth immediately," said Neuromate, thanking Antimatter and rushing to CuberApp. They could barely talk as the thought of Mastermind awakening again gave them a chill down the spine with unlimited frightening possibilities.

The underwater gathering place was still the same and everyone was safe, at least uptil now. They were going to break the deadliest news to all of them.

"As we, the human helping apps were happy with a sweeping response and were rejoicing, the disintegrating, diminutive variable Mastermind probably diverged himself as infinitesimal fractions and escaped through the miniscule spaces in the mathematical equation prison, only to converge again somewhere in the universe."

"It is impossible," said the Quad on hearing what they saw at GAIA BH2 and were utterly upset with the whole situation as they blamed themselves for being overconfident.

"Well, we should now think that there is a possibility that he could escape that prison, and we should think ahead," said Neuromate.

"Yes, the opponent should never be considered weak, especially if it is Mastermind," said DoctorApp.

Helix and Paper were back with their results and they could link everything to SJ's lab computer.

"Can he attach to a human?" asked HackApp.

"We don't know about his capabilities," said DoctorApp.

"Let's consider all possibilities," said Chap.

"We could locate the ultimate Codepod to be in a dark zone with a lot of heat around but the sound doesn't match any of the places in the universe we have been," said Infinity.

"It is an unusual sound though," said Shunya.

"If he has attached to SJ, he can very well build another Neuromate easily," said Neuromate, saddened.

"But he will not have the baby app with the App intent you have, Neuromate," said Shunya, *"that is of utmost importance for app development and for an app to achieve what he or she desires."*

"What should we do?" asked Neuromate.

"Well we have hacked all other files and data on that computer," said HackApp, calling everyone as Chap was on the computer screen to display what they found.

The faculty also were ready with their analysis and suggested that one of the equation in the prison cell may have been partially solved, which could have led to a discontinuity in the bars and let Mastermind escape. It seemed that all the missing pieces were falling into place. Neuromate was disheartened as Mastermind attached to his creator and he will have to fight SJ now.

As Neuromate was lost in his thoughts for a while, DoctorApp shook him. *"It is not SJ he attached to,"* said DoctorApp.

The files of the computer were getting displayed showing corrupted and bugged files, when Recorder, Counsellor and Environ came. They had seen the recordings of the gathering. *"There is no mole amongst us,"* said Counsellor.

"All of us behaved appropriately," said Environ.

"Only the outsider was different," said Recorder, and everyone turned to him, *"It is Neurolink."*

The files which were corrupted, all were the installation process of Neurolink.

As Recorder played the clip when she left the party saying she is unwell, she had a crooked smile and she logged on remotely to the SJ's computer to upload the video of the Ultimate Codepod.

"If Mastermind is with her, he has access to SJ's brain anyhow. We need to stop him," said Neuromate, worried.

"And we need to find the ultimate Codepod," said the Quad.

"Before he freezes all of us here, let's assign tasks and leave this place," suggested Facelook.

"But where to go?" asked Noflix.

"Let's have a plan. We can't act randomly," said Neuromate, *"I feel the Quad, Shunya, Infinity and the faculty should search for the ultimate Codepod and run the destruction program as soon as it is found. We all on Earth will divide into teams with CuberApp, PickApp and Environ taking care of quick transportation to locate the remote possibility of it being on Earth. Myself, DoctorApp and Counsellor will go to SJ's lab to find Neurolink and try to show that we still don't know that Mastermind is attached to her. We will use our tricks to get him come out on his own."*

"I think it is a perfect plan," said Shunya, *"I just wanted to tell you one thing as I know him inside out. He might be the custodian of the being he gets attached to, but there is reciprocal transmission in phases of his weakness, when the mind of the captive takes over. All the good things he did in part were whenever he felt weak that he won't be able to accomplish what he desired for, I took over and made him do things which were better for apps. So probably you need to look for such a moment and direct Neurolink to act smart. She can listen to each and everything you speak, she can only act when she gets the opportunity."*

"That's brilliant," said Infinity, feeling proud.

"It sounds like a Dissociative Identity Disorder to me," said DoctorApp.

"That's how it presents, like a duality," said Shunya.

All dispersed with a lightning speed with an ultimate goal to defeat Mastermind once and for all.

As Neuromate reached SJ's lab, he was stunned to see SJ with Neurolink inside him, instructing him. Neurolink was clearly altered because of the attached Mastermind and so was SJ. They were ready to destroy anyone who came their way. SJ was having immense power, both physically and mentally.

Neuromate wanted to do as Shunya had said, just talk to Neurolink so that she could listen to him.

"Neurolink, we know it is not your fault. It's Mastermind, and he has attached himself to you, altering your behaviour. He is doing all this to achieve what he wants. SJ developed my initial codes and he needs them to put it in the ultimate Codepod to make another Neuromate who will act according to him and let him control humans as well as other apps," said Neuromate amidst numerous attacks from SJ to destroy him.

He was not sure whether she heard him or not, but SJ did not stop.

While Counsellor and DoctorApp were trying to save themselves too, DoctorApp suddenly had a flash of thought, *"If Shunya knows so much, as Mastermind was basically possessing him, he must be knowing where the ultimate Codepod is."* whispered DoctorApp.

"It didn't occur to me, yes you are right. He said that he knew Mastermind inside out," said Neuromate.

"Is he still under Mastermind's influence?" asked a confused Counsellor.

"Don't know, but we need to connect with the Quad," said Neuromate.

They were trying to save themselves from the violent attacks of SJ guided by corrupted Neurolink. Neuromate just reached out to SJ's computer and logged in easily as he knew the passcode. Counsellor and DoctorApp shielded him while he ran the program to uninstall Neurolink. That would make SJ bedbound with paralysis again but set his mind free.

He was impatient while the program was running and all the data linked to Neurolink was getting erased completely when SJ gave a final blow while pulling the system away and threw it on the ground.

Neurolink fainted and DoctorApp went ahead to help her. SJ fell to the ground confirming that Neuromate could accomplish what he was doing. He transferred him on the couch with the help of Counsellor.

Mr Deduction and Ms Analysis barged in hurriedly and spoke in broken phrases, trying to catch breath.

"We have reached to a conclusion that Shunya can't be unaware of where the ultimate Codepod is. We have suspicion that he is hiding something as he didn't mention about the whereabouts and all of us are searching for it like crazy."

While all the teams showed up one by one, not been able to find the ultimate Codepod, Neuromate decided to travel to GAIA BH2 and tell the Quad about it.

"But she is sill unconscious. And we don't know if she wakes up to be under Mastermind's influence. We will be doomed," said DoctorApp.

"Let's take her along then," said Neuromate.

"It is very unsafe. As we are not sure what Mastermind is capable of," said the Counsellor.

"Doc, can't you keep her sedated?" asked Environ.

"Sure I can, but she is not just an app, she is a chip like a hardware, and Mastermind is a number. So I don't know how effective my sedation will be on them as they are different species," said DoctorApp.

"I think we have no other choice," said Neuromate, instructing CuberApp to take all of them to GAIA BH2.

Antimatter was in IOA, taking care and told them that others were still away looking for the Codepod.

"Where is Shunya?" asked Neuromate.

"He wasn't feeling too well, so he decided to stay back in his chamber while others are scanning the universe," said Antimatter.

"Let me go to him," said Neuromate, explaining the situation to Antimatter, *"all others along with Neurolink will be safe with you. When the Quad and Infinity return, please tell them to join me."*

"But what should we do with her?" asked Counsellor, pointing at Neurolink.

"I clearly don't have an answer to that, but I presume continuing sedation is the only option. I feel I should get answers by then," said Neuromate.

Neuromate started walking towards the chamber Antimatter told Shunya was in. While moving, he was trying to think of the various possibilities. What could Shunya be hiding and why? Is Mastermind still attached to Neurolink? When he didn't find Mastermind in the cell, it clearly indicated that he had escaped. Where is he right now? All the baffling questions were making him squirm with uncertainty and fear. But he gathered himself and went ahead as that was the only missing piece which only Shunya could solve.

The Chamber was a tight enclosed rhombicosidodecahedron bound by equational bars. He could not see any other way of entering except for solving the equations. He felt that the Quad could be of help at this moment as he himself was not a math genius. He tried moving around the structure to see if there was any possibility he could get in.

To his utmost surprise, one of the bars slid to accommodate his entry into the enormous dark space. Shunya was inside but couldn't be seen.

"Can you hear me Shunya?" called out Neuromate.

"Yes I can," said Shunya, lighting up the space to reveal the most high tech lab.

"How are you feeling?"

"I am good. What brings you here? Could you track the Codepod and get rid of Mastermind?"

"No, no, that's why I am here. There is something which I felt you must be knowing unless Mastermind made you sleep while he did it."

"What?"

"Where the ultimate Codepod is? Because he was still attached to you when he hid it. So you must have seen it."

"I would have told you if I knew it. I am upset that you doubted me."

"Oh no, we just thought.... Well leave it. I am sorry that I disturbed you."

"Where is Neurolink?"

"She is here with us."

"Us? Means you have others here too?"

"Yes, we all are here, thinking that we will get final answers from you."

"Ohhh... so still we could not locate it."

"No."

"And is Mastermind still attached to her?"

"We don't know."

They both were pondering what could be done next, when the Quad and Infinity arrived with no news of the ultimate Codepod, and met Antimatter, who briefed them about the developments.

"Why didn't it occur to any of us? Clearly Shunya must be knowing it and he hid it," said the Quad angrily.

"Maybe there is something else," said Infinity, defending Shunya.

"Well, Neuromate has gone to talk to him," said Antimatter.

"But what if he is still under Mastermind's influence? I have stopped believing anyone now," said DoctorApp.

"I think we should let Neurolink get up and see what she says," said Counsellor.

"And we should go see Neuromate," said the Quad, *"he might be in danger."*

"Myself and doc can take care of Neurolink," said Antimatter, *"you all should go."*

"Let everyone be here in another enclosure," said the Quad, instructing the Mathematics and Sciences faculty to make an unsolvable equations prison around themselves and everyone, except

Antimatter, Neurolink and DoctorApp. The Quad alongwith Infinity quickly moved towards Shunya's chamber.

Neurolink was getting awake as the sedation waned off. As she got up to be at an unfamiliar place, she was puzzled. DoctorApp took care and helped her get up.

"Where am I? And who is this?" asked Neurolink.

"He is Antimatter and we are in GAIA BH2," said DoctorApp, trying to assess her behaviour.

"Ohh, I came to the party and felt so unwell that I had to leave. I don't remember anything thereafter. I think I blacked out," said Neurolink.

DoctorApp could still not rule out Mastermind playing games with them, but she sounded genuine.

"Come, let's take you somewhere safe," said Antimatter.

"Why? What happened?" asked Neurolink.

As DoctorApp and Antimatter explained the sequence of events to her, she was more than shocked. She was worried for SJ too.

They decided to take her along and join the Quad and Infinity. They did not want to risk leaving her there, still unsure about her.

The rhombicosidodecahedron was a puzzle chamber with so much to solve to be able to enter. As the Quad were in the process of sliding the equational bars, the trio joined them and explained them about Neurolink's blackout. They just thought of focusing on entering inside first and think about other things later.

One bar finally gave way and they were inside the dark space.

Shunya lit it up and hugged Infinity.

"Where is Neuromate?" asked DoctorApp.

"Who? Neuromate? He never came here," said Shunya.

"He came to this chamber. I only sent him here and I saw him entering. That's when I left my gaze on him," said Antimatter.

"Why are you lying? Where is he? And is Mastermind here too?" asked the Quad.

"Finally, I think it is time for you all to face the truth," started Shunya, *"Everyone is here. Within my complex geometric hideout. And so is your ultimate Codepod."* He signalled the Codepod to rise and be visible to everyone. Neuromate was inside the Codepod, though unattached to the portal.

"What are you doing brother? Where is Mastermind? Has he got you again?" asked Infinity, coming closer to him, *"Talk to me, please."*

Shunya shrugged Infinity away. He was speaking in Mastermind's voice now. *"Brother? Is that what you really feel for Shunya? When everyone was praising you for being the largest, the most abundant, you were getting elated, while your own brother was called 'nothing'. The nothingness was killing him from within. He sometimes thought he was the best mathematical figure but no one seemed to value him. He was sent from place to place, used by everyone for their own advantage, but never got the appreciation he deserved. The apps are enjoying fame and money, but he was left as he was, always. Kicked into a corner, isolated, lonely and depressed. You think I went to him? No, he came to me for help."*

"What are you doing with Neuromate?" asked DoctorApp.

"What he deserves. Just a slight change and he will act as I want," replied Mastermind.

"Don't do this," said Infinity.

"You all have not left me with any choice," said Mastermind.

"This all is very confusing. How could you get away from the prison? And then you were with Neurolink?" asked the Quad.

Mastermind started laughing loudly.

"We can take Shunya out again, as we did then. We just need to expose AntiShunya," said Infinity.

"Laughing, "You could not decipher it, geniuses?" said Mastermind, *"What will you take out? It is I, me, myself. You locked me well last time, but then brought me out yourself."*

"What?" said Antimatter, confused.

"Shunya is Mastermind and Mastermind is Shunya," shouted Neuromate from inside the Codepod.

"Well, the secret is out," said Shunya, *"brother, I am sorry if I disappointed you, but I assumed this variable mind to fight with my situation. And look, how successful I am. I started IOA, I made remarkable apps, I defeated your favourite Quad many times and above all, I developed Neuromate, my first step to control the human world." Shunya laughed loudly. "And Neurolink was just a short trip to program her for devastation, nothing else. My variable mind then was back again with my constant mind."*

"So you are a dissociative personality indeed," said DoctorApp.

"And I can physically dissociate it to go to another being as well," said Shunya, *"I want the world to realize how powerful I am."*

As Shunya was elaborating about his achievements and indulged and engrossed in his thoughts, the Quad quietly slipped towards the Codepod and set Neuromate free. They then started the destruction program which was going to take some time, but they had to be away to avoid getting hurt.

"There is only one way to stop him," said Neuromate, *"ask Antimatter to expose AntiShunya and engulf him, once we know that there is no existence of Mastermind as a separate variable. It is just him."*

"But engulfing Shunya means a lot. He will be out of the universe. Can you imagine a world without zero? Leave alone the calculations, theorems and data, even the apps will fall apart," said the Quad.

"Can't he be discovered again?" asked Neuromate.

"We don't know, but we can try this as there is no other option," said the Quad, *"and we need to leave this chamber soon as this Codepod is going to explode."*

While the Quad moved to Antimatter, Neuromate stood in front of Shunya.

"Mastermind alias Shunya alias Zero, your game is over. You will be finished and so will be your dream," said Neuromate.

"The ultimate Codepod is going to blow up your chamber very soon," said the Quad.

Shunya was slightly disturbed, but then laughed, *" I can build it again. I have the blueprint of your invention, didn't you think about that?"*

"But how will you build it when you are not there anymore?" said Antimatter exposing AntiShunya to suck in Shunya in no time.

They all ran to leave the chamber and came out to head towards the IOA structure where all the apps were in the equational prison. They were becoming disfigured and dysfunctional with the absence of Shunya. As the chamber exploded, they could not believe that they had achieved what they wanted. They asked all of them to come out and briefed them about the final outcome. While all apps were unable to retain their form, the faculty helped them come out.

"So what should we do next?" asked Antimatter, seeing the critical condition of the apps.

"I think you should spit out Shunya now. We can only hope that he comes out in pure form, without a variable mind. It will be his rebirth. If there is any doubt, you can suck him in again," said Neuromate in a frail voice.

"Let's do this Antimatter," said Infinity.

Shunya came out to be part of the universe again. He was the initiator of everything. There was nothing before the Big Bang and it was only him. Maybe over the time, people forgot about his importance and value, which made him plan for a revenge, but things became better again. For the fraction of time he was away, everyone felt his absence and the world started falling apart, but his rebirth made the universe the same again.

As all the apps regained strength, they were ready to travel back to the Earth and said goodbye to the faculty, the Quad, Antimatter, Infinity and Shunya.

Neuromate had a long journey ahead. To be the first app in history to connect with humans at neural level, and be their real mate.

Epilogue

The new era continued with the improved quality of life of humans, albeit elevation of apps as supreme superpower with humans inadvertently completely dependent on them. It was still a mystery whether Shunya came out in pure form or the same form, and Neuromate was still suspicious. What lies in the future, was unpredictable and the truth was to be unravelled soon...

Volume 2 : Appology: The Calculated Clue

About the Author

Dr. Anurakti Dev Singla (maiden Srivastava) is an interventional pediatric and fetal cardiologist and electrophysiologist with a strong literary inclination. She has published her award winning Hindi poetry book "Aatman" before and has few short stories and snippets to her credit apart from her international professional research publications and contributions to medical books. This novel is her first step into the world of scientific fiction. Though she had the storyline in her mind for a long time, it could finally take shape now.

9 789334 014525

Printed at Repro India Ltd.